Widowmaker

Widowmaker

William Appel

Walker and Company
New York

This one is for Denise
They're all for Denise now.

And for Nicholas
For whom I've never changed a diaper
or warmed a bottle yet I'm lucky enough
to have as family.

First published in the United States of America in 1994
by Walker Publishing Company, Inc.

Published simultaneously in Canada by Thomas Allen & Son
Canada, Limited, Markham, Ontario

Library of Congress Cataloging-in-Publication Data
Appel, William.
Widowmaker: / William Appel.
p.   cm.
ISBN 0-8027-3193-7
I. Title.
PS3551.P556W5   1994
813'.54—dc20   94-15362
CIP

Printed in the United States of America
2 4 6 8 10 9 7 5 3 1

"Each of us is a crowd."
—Piero Ferrucci,
What We May Be

Acknowledgments

As always, from my first novel through to the one I'm writing now, my cousin Sandra has been at my side giving relentless TLC and wise criticism. Once again, thanks Sandra.

Constant too has been the generous support and technical advice from Denis Walsh—healer, scientist, teacher, and writer.

And special thanks to all those people I'm fortunate enough to have whose support helps me bear with the creases in life: Rose Appel, Ben and Barbara Aliza, Mark and Karen Weiss, Marilyn and Steve Pessin, Paul Cassidy, Marie DeVito, Marlene Sherer, Alan and Joyce Reed, Brugeleh and J.M., Frank Hayes, Ken Munroe, Yvonne Murray, Barbara Donhauser, Gail and Jack Bushardt, and Abe and Charlotte Berman.

Many thanks to Michael Seidman, who is without question the finest editor I've had the pleasure of working with.

And *merci* to Philip who is not only an expert on crime fiction but a gentleman in the highest sense of the word.

I owe a special debt of gratitude to Pat Kozma and Executary, the best manuscript preparation service in the universe.

And thank you Jack Youngman for being the greatest fan any writer could hope for.

1

Her need for another mission was now so intense that not even memories of the ones who had gasped and convulsed could lessen it.

First, though, she must prepare the special powder.

She raced to the rear of her Lexington Avenue apartment, past art deco and art nouveau butting against high-tech brushed metals and Lucite. The chairs were slung leather, the tables glass and chrome. Each room was a different shade of red foil wallpaper. The air smelled of eucalyptus and jasmine.

Inside the miniature greenhouse in her garden she chose a few large specimens of fragrant white lily of the valley. How deceivingly sweet the drooping, bell-shaped flowers were.

Under squares of fluorescents in the kitchen she chopped off the roots. Flung them into a Cuisinart. The resulting powder weighed just a little over four grams. She had become expert at guessing how many roots made one tablespoon.

She poured the powder into a microwave dish, then chose a setting of 4. She watched the invisible alchemy. Imagined a crystallization to full potency in each granule of powder.

When she was sure the powder was thoroughly dried, she carefully poured it into the sterling pillbox she used exclusively for this purpose. For a glorious instant she heard the pleadings of the last one as she watched him, balled up on the soaked sheets, pink spittle bursting from his lips.

She put her miniature tape recorder and the special

cassette she used for these occasions in her unborn-calfskin handbag. Jammed in the condoms and the surgical gloves. As always, she saved the crisp twenty-dollar bill for last. She savored folding it into the shape of a traditional lapel handkerchief.

The inside of her thighs quivered now. Her lungs felt pressed flat.

She sat in the sauna till she felt she'd been peeled and her quick exposed. She drew water into the whirlpool, pouring in an extract of the ambergris secreted by sperm whales, which softens and silkens the skin. She lay trying to conjure up ones she'd had in the past. She could remember few of them with any accuracy, and even those kept looming into focus and fading out again. When she tried to picture them she saw a kind of hybrid: this one's eyes and that one's mouth and another's tears. Only the afterbliss remained.

Soon she applied a mud mask. Rubbed away dead skin from elbows and feet.

She removed the hardened mask and splashed herself with icy astringent. Creamed her entire body.

At her mirrored dressing table she chose an auburn wig and adjusted it on her head. Inserted a pair of green contacts.

The first time came swimming up out of her memory with vivid clarity. How, afterward, everything had been changed. Where she was then, she had never been before. She had trembled, and it had been as though the sky, the street, people, had been birthed out of the very air only a moment ago.

She wrapped her fingernails and painted them with four coats of French enamel the color of a courtesan's garter she'd once seen in a painting. From vials and jars and tubes so suggestively packaged they seemed part of the process of seduction, she selected tints and blushers and glosses and shadows and applied them with brushes sleek as otter fur.

When she had finished she gazed into the glass. Her lips parted at her artistry. Her hair was a thick, soft prism. Beneath shadow and longer and fuller lashes, her eyes appeared twice their size. The whites were white as refrigerator gloss, the irises liquid with promise and taunting caprice. Her mouth was pouty, lips glistening and inviting.

She rouged her nipples. Selected a perfume of bergamot and doe musk, precious as virgin's milk. Daubed the scent between her breasts, at her temples, and behind her knees. In her completely mirrored bedroom she chose a low-cut black dress of silk fine as smoke. Around her neck she wore a sterling chain-mail necklace that defied any man to test her armor.

It was six forty-five when Carmina hailed a taxi to begin her mission.

Carmina ate at a table where she had a view of the entire Biarritz Hotel bar. Dinner alone, she knew, made a woman who might appear to be a prostitute seem a businesswoman from out of town.

Afterward she sat at the bar, which was crowded with men. Middle-aged salesmen with whiskey showing in the veins in their faces. Bald men with stomachs like sacks of groceries. Old men with irises like lumps of jellied poultry fat. Young men with fluffy, newly cut hair—even their eyebrows looked cleaned and pressed.

So many. Each a possibility that excited her. The random collision of prey and hunter. They were always so predictable. Their standard lie was that they were not married. Or married but separated. Or in an open marriage. Or married but not getting along with their wives. Or . . . or . . . or . . .

Studying them all, she felt like a panther prowling through strong moonlight, disguised as a beautiful and cunning woman.

She purposely radiated an air of languor mixed with impatience, assurance, and brazenness. In the set of her mouth there was a trace of challenge—even hostility. She knew what the fools wanted.

She sat on the edge of the barstool, on the edge of everything, waiting.

In moments the man she waited for arrived, wearing a light blue shirt, white pants, and a blue blazer with an embroidered gold anchor over the breast pocket. Middle-aged sailor boy tonight, she thought.

Shifting seductively on the barstool, Carmina gave him her bold, sexy smile, which worked all the better for its deliberateness.

He immediately strutted over, at once cocksure and edgy. His tie had a pattern of little whales. He twitched his horrible pubic mustache.

"You alone?" he said.

"I hope not anymore."

He hadn't recognized her. She felt as pleased as a child who has been given something precious to play with.

"Want a drink?"

"Why not?"

He smiled, showing his straight but corn-colored teeth. His eyes, though a lovely shade of blue, were dead as coat buttons. Like the others before him, his desire was obvious in the strained whiteness between his eyes.

He waved at the bartender, then ordered.

"What's your name?"

"Carmina."

"Italiano, huh? How long you here? Where from?"

"Rome—nine years," she lied. "What's your name?"

"Peter. Uh . . . Peter Masters."

She smiled. They rarely gave their real last names. But, as in this case, the first names they offered were usually genuine. He was wearing the sly hooky-player smile they usually wore at this stage. She glanced at his left hand, saw the wedding band, and was reminded that he was married. Peter. What a perfect name for him. Prick.

Their drinks arrived. Out of the corner of her eye she saw a man who looked as if he'd never been a child take in what he could of the naked tops of her breasts, stealing the sight from Peter "Masters" as though it were gold.

"You look mysterious, you know?"

"How do you mean?"

"Like Rita Hayworth in *Gilda*."

"Must have been before my time."

"Don't remind me. Glamorous. You know."

"Smoldering?" She looked directly into his eyes, savoring his hunger.

"That's it!"

A passing man paused, smiled at her, then looked at her breasts. His eyes moved down to the waistband of her dress, then followed the seam down to where it went out of sight.

She turned to the man who called himself Peter Masters. "You live in New York?" As if she didn't know.

"Jersey. Got the largest pet shop in Essex County. Sell more tropical fish than anyone in New York."

He was so comically earnest she could hardly keep a straight face. She let him crow and puff, parading his accomplishments like a schoolboy giving a summary of his turns at bat. She allowed him the foolish assumption his possessions would be a measure of his worth to her.

She delighted in the way he opened up like a sprung leak because of her nodding and faked awe. It was marvelous to string him along, with his braggart's poses and exaggerations. She would like to dump broken glass into his little boy's crotch.

She could see the fool was wondering if she were a hooker. He might be too frightened to go with a woman who wasn't. She leaned over and whispered in his ear.

"Just because I'm a working girl, don't think I don't choose my men."

She could almost feel his muscles relax.

"Sure, I understand."

"Why don't we have a drink—someplace cozier? What's your room number?"

"Four twenty-nine."

"I'll go to the ladies' room. Wait ten minutes before you go up. I'll meet you there. Be a doll and order us some drinks?" She rolled the lobe of his ear insinuatingly. "Mmm . . . I feel like slipping my tongue between the buttons of your shirt."

He said breathlessly, "We didn't discuss, uh . . .
business."

"I get a hundred."

"Fine."

She rose, feeling men's eyes on her as she slunk promis-
ingly away. She felt more naked than if she were nude. Her
buttocks burned as if spat on. *Yearn, you bastards, yearn.*

When she arrived at his door he reached out his hands.
They were cool and damp, like cold buttered toast.

Inside she said, "Let me change first. You turn around
now like a good boy, and close your eyes."

When he did, she took out her pillbox and deftly poured
the powdered crystals into his drink. Then she pulled a
diaphanous peach teddy from her handbag and changed.

"You can turn around now," she said finally.

He turned red at the sight of her.

"Let's have our scotches first," she said, and watched him
hurry his final drink. His heat was making his hair curl.

"Maybe," she said, "you'd relax better if we danced a little,
huh?"

"Sure, anything you say."

She took her small cassette recorder from her handbag and
turned it on.

> *. . . Fem-me-na, tu si na ma-la fem-me-na*
> *Chist 'uo-cchie'e fat-to . . .*

"Waltz?" she said holding her arms out. "I love music you
can dance close to. Puts me in the mood."

He gave his hands to her. She pulled him to her till she
could feel with her thighs where his flesh had risen.

> *Fem-me-na, si tu peg-gio'e na vi-pa-ra*
> *me'e 'ntus-se-ca-ta . . .*

After a time she stole a look at her Bulgari watch.
Visualized the crystals inside him doing their magic. Just a
little while longer . . .

He fumbled with the tongue of his belt to free the pointed

metal prong. Carefully, he lowered his Jockey briefs over the head of his small penis. She was repulsed by its crookedness, its curve to the right.

He had a girdle of fat at his waist and plump little breasts. No matter. What he would soon give her far transcended whatever ugliness she had to endure.

He climbed on the bed and lay with his hands folded on his breast like a child being good. Blood welled up in her eyes. She came over, kissed his lips. Kissed him till his penis beat against her belly.

His fingers drew at her breasts as though sex had to be pulled from a woman.

She ran her nails up and down and under his scythe-shaped tube till it throbbed. She slipped the condom on. Then she climbed above him and impaled herself. She could smell whiskey and smoke each time he breathed out.

As he thrust up she pretended desire was making her bite his shoulder and glanced at her watch. Just a few moments more . . .

She let him roll her over. She could feel his steel-wool mustache and disgusting slippery lips on her neck. She drew on him with her inner muscles.

"You'd like to drain me dry, wouldn't you?" he said.

"And you'd like to get so deep inside, you'd bust right through. But you know you can't get very far. Why do you keep trying?"

"P-please?" A lopsided smile.

"Again."

"Pretty please?"

"Not cute enough."

"Pleeease?"

"Good boy."

Feeling a pride—as if she had fashioned her body by herself—she let go. Let him dip in and out. Twirl sideways. Then plunge ahead. *"Here,"* she commanded, "and *here."*

When he came his teeth clenched and ground together. He moved back from her.

"Bet-ter, baby?" Then, "What's wrong?"

"N-nothing."

"Guilty, huh?"

"She's a wonderful wife and mother. Very religious. But sex is—"

"Boring?"

"I would *never* call it that. Could never talk to her like we did, though. Think it was dirty. She's the best, but—"

He bent over, motionless.

"You all right?"

"D-don't know. Feel funny. Prob'ly just excited."

He stayed bent over as if waiting. Then his palm moved of its own accord to his chest.

"My h-heart," he said hollowly. "No air. Jesus!"

"I'll get you some water."

Suddenly he had fallen off the bed, doubled up on the floor.

"S-queezing my heart. Scared. Doctor, please!"

"And spoil my fun, Mr. Giannini?"

His head shot up then, eyes bulging. How she loved their final astonished look, like an animal realizing it had blundered into a net.

She ran the bathwater and turned on the TV so that his attempts at shouting couldn't be heard. Then she fixed a drink and made herself comfortable to enjoy his writhing and groaning. Checked her watch. Only minutes more. She looked at the pile of his clothes by the bed. They seemed to be waiting to be outlined in chalk.

When he lay perfectly still, she pulled on the surgical gloves. Examined the corpse and the room fastidiously for all traces of herself. Then examined them again.

Before leaving she took the specially folded twenty-dollar bill and stuck it into the lapel pocket of his blazer. There was, as always, a sweet melancholy, as if some haunting tune had just faded on the air.

Outside in the commonplace world the summer sky was a pale shade of indigo. Carmina Rivincita thought she had never seen anything so lovely in her life. How gaily the little flags were fluttering and snapping on the hotel battlements. Seeing a firefly, she imagined it making a drowsy sound that was the very voice of summer. Parked cars basked under the sodium glare. Others scudded along sleek as seals. The people among whom she moved were strange to her. She was not of their species. Her eyes were scorched, and there was an ache in the small of her back that told her she was exhausted. Yet she refused to consider sleep. She might have been a child arriving home after a day of wild activity.

Suddenly she felt famished and thought, it's the executioner who eats a hearty breakfast! She wished she could stay awake all night, full of her sleepy, lighthearted fulfillment.

Tomorrow would be a glorious day. Oh yes, glorious.

▽

2

" . . . AND IN MARCH Bermuda's skies are even clearer than now," said Josh Berman, New York City's former medical examiner.

"No kidding," said his wife, Kate, smiling. "Have we ever gone anywhere when you weren't convinced that another season was the best time of year for viewing? Thanks, Donelle."

The housekeeper, a black woman with green eyes and ginger hair, had just set a large tray down on the dining room table where they sat. Yellow jam was spread on a stack of steaming whole wheat toast. A porcelain teapot covered with a gay cozy held English breakfast tea. Bananas the size of a child's fingers were bunched around palmetto dates.

"I'm so glad we chose this house instead of a hotel," Josh said, looking at the high-backed Chippendale chairs, small rugs, and British antiques. "No TV, no phones, no people. I love Casey, but I'm not unhappy he couldn't make it."

Kate studied him. The little banana he peeled looked even tinier in his huge hand. His recent tan accentuated the contrast between his latent power and his gentleness. At fifty-two he still carried himself like the athlete he had been, despite being a dozen pounds overweight.

Kate poured tea. "Casey wanted to be alone with this new woman in his life."

"Maybe. But I think his weird new murder case kept him home as much as anything." He noticed the laugh lines on her face, which made her seem more precious to him than ever. He bit into a piece of toast. "Mmmm. What is this?"

"Loquat jam. Kind of a cross between kumquat and pear. What's so bizarre about his new case?"

"Have any idea how gorgeous you look with that tan against that white tube top?"

"That won't work."

"Go fool a criminologist."

"What's bizarre?"

"No shoptalk. We promised, 'member?"

"Right," she said, sounding relieved. "Okay, so what was so special about the Bermuda sky last night?"

He set his cup down quickly. "First, they've got a hell of an astronomy club here. Good telescope, too. I saw all of Scorpio. Home, the bottom of the tail can't be seen."

"What else?"

"Centauri, which you can't see at all from New York, and—"

"Telegram," Donelle said, entering.

Kate opened the envelope and read aloud:

DECIDED TAKE YOU UP VACATION STOP
ARRIVE WITH NORA TODAY STOP BUY
YOU A DRINK STOP CASEY

"Very disappointed?" Kate said.

"No. Except I was really enjoying having you all to myself."

"So, is that as close as you're going to get?"

Smiling, he followed her into their bedroom.

▽

3

NINA AWOKE UNABLE to account for the bizarre and
impossible condition in which she found herself.

An alluring scent of unfamiliar perfume clung to her. In
her mouth was the dry taste of ashes, though she had never
smoked.

What had she done this time? Where had she been? For
how long? A moment? A day? She made the sign of the cross.

She had learned painfully and thoroughly over the years
that she could not answer such questions. She looked at the
clock on the nightstand. 8:05 A.M. She had nearly an hour
before her trucks started rolling.

She looked at her calendar nervously. This was the day
she would finally meet Ralph Weir. In the letters he sent in
response to her personals ad he sounded so sweet, so caring,
that a flower of hope had bloomed in her heart. Maybe,
finally, she had found someone to make up for all her
loneliness and disappointment. She'd never had any problem dealing with men in business, but once there was even
a hint of the romantic she became excruciatingly shy. Now,
however, Ralph had stirred up a warm, almost sensuous
thrill of expectancy.

She lay for a moment longer, conscious of the rough male
hug of the blanket. She needed weight to sleep, even now
with July temperatures.

Though Nina was tall, straight, and in her mid-thirties,
she made her way through the house like a stooped old
woman. The rooms were decorated with flecked maroon

wallpaper, red pile rugs, heavy, dark, ornate furniture.

In the study she lifted the silver-framed photograph of her parents that sat next to a miniature of Sicily's scarlet-and-gold flag on the desk that had been her father's. Her face was an amalgam of theirs. Her mother's high cheekbones and hooded, milk-chocolate eyes. Her father's firm chin and flesh the color of bronze. When she looked in a mirror she saw a familiar puzzle that had been put together wrong.

She kept the study spotless, but there was a sense of things left standing far too long in the same place. The air felt dull, as if one of its vital essences had been used up long ago. Nina's aura was not unlike the study's. The sum of her fine bone structure, bronze complexion, large eyes, dark curly hair and slim, well-proportioned figure wasn't sultriness— even attractiveness. Instead her severely pulled back hair, makeup-free face, dull eyes, and loose, drab clothing made her plain. She was like a stale floral arrangement whose flowers had not yet begun to die but had lost some of their color. She lacked intensity, and any consciousness of her own potential appeal.

Her excitement about meeting Ralph beginning to turn to apprehension, she hurried to the kitchen, which always prompted her fondest memories. It was here, in the cheeriest room of the house, the family had always gathered to talk. In the morning light the room had a scrubbed, eager aspect. She would not be surprised if her father appeared, young and handsome, smiling to wish her good morning. How could she be apprehensive here?

Still, memories of blind dates who never phoned her afterward, singles gatherings and dances where she'd never been spoken to, computer dating services that never made a match for her, sucked the air from the room. She felt fragile as an icicle. Even the strands of her hair felt like slender stalactites of crystal. Just the continuous ringing of the silence might break her.

"Hey, Nina," she heard her father say, "remember you're a Benanti."

Straightening her shoulders, she made her way to the bedroom to dress.

When she heard the first truck revving she unlocked her upper Sentry lock and lower Yale lock and safety chain and removed the chrome-plated bar braced under the doorknob. Dressed in the kind of white lab coat Poppa had insisted all employees wear, she walked the few steps down Washington Street to Pesce International.

Despite the gentrification of the West Village, there were a few remaining warehouses. Pesce International was one.

"Yo, Nina!" one of her drivers called. She waved back. The roar of motors and filters made her shout to be heard. Although the warehouse was air-conditioned, the evaporation of the water in thousands of Pesce aquariums gave it a tropical humidity.

She opened the door to her office, which had once been her father's. As usual Poppa's old secretary, Graziela, brought her a mug of coffee with a list of the day's bills of lading. She was a tiny woman with a sheep's muzzle for a nose.

"You heard or what?" Graziela said.

"What?"

"Peter Giannini. Found him dead in a room at that fancy Biarritz Hotel. Heart attack. Must have been with a woman. What a disgrace for his wife and kids."

"Jesus God. Are you sure?"

"Look at me."

Nina looked into the phlegm-colored eyes and crossed herself. Of all her customers, she had liked Peter the least. Once she had accidentally overheard him bragging to one of her drivers that while his wife slept in a hotel he sneaked down to the bar, picked up a prostitute, and took her to another room in the hotel. Afterward he slept with his wife. There was a word in Italian for men like Peter—*schivazzo*. Still, she felt terrible for him. Even worse for his wife and kids. "Send a mass card. Also flowers to the funeral home."

Nina let Graziela rant for a few more moments about the

disgrace Peter had left as a legacy. Then she excused herself, saying she needed to get on with the bills of lading. The truth was, she found even the mention of a heart attack disturbing; a heart attack had killed her father.

Graziela left with a frustrated expression bordering on impertinence. Nina would have let the woman go years ago if not for Graziela's loyalty to her parents.

Angelo Benanti's business had flourished mainly because he was skilled at breeding species of tropical fishes that few others—in some cases no one else—could breed. When Nina's mother took over the business after his death, she tried to compensate for his loss by hiring some of the country's best breeders. But none had ability approaching Angelo's.

When Nina inherited the business after her mother's death five years ago, she had been shocked to find it close to bankruptcy. Asian fish breeders' prices were so low that most American breeders, like her mother, could not compete.

Nina had decided to stop the breeding entirely. She let the high-salaried breeders on the payroll go and had all her fishes shipped in from the Far East.

Then she offered a service no one had thought to give.

Pet shop owners outside New York City had to visit the Manhattan wholesalers on an average of once a week to purchase fishes, an inconvenience and expense. Also, these owners lost a great deal to pilferage when they were absent from their businesses. Nina's trucks delivered right to their shops. The dealers were willing to pay premium prices to Nina because of their savings in time and money. The business was now eight times the size of the one her father had left her mother, and Nina was an immensely wealthy woman.

Nina tried to look over the accounts receivable, but soon her fear of meeting Ralph Weir stole her concentration.

She went over to the aquarium containing her pet starfish. The sea star fascinated her. She took a book from the top of her desk and opened it to an article by a Dr. S. P. Monks, a passage she had read so many times she could almost recite it. Monks's words, strangely, seemed written for her.

I am inclined to think that Phateria . . . always breaks itself, no matter what may be the impulse. They make breaks when conditions are changed, sometimes within a few hours after being placed in jars. . . . Whatever may be the stimulus, the animal can and does break of itself. . . . The ordinary method is for the main portion of the starfish to remain fixed and passive with the tube feet set on the side of the departing ray, and for this ray to walk slowly away at right angles to the body, to change position, twist, and do all the active labor necessary to the breakage.

There was also a comment by marine biologist Ed Ricketts:

It would seem that in an animal that deliberately pulls itself apart we have the very acme of something or other.

How wonderful it would be if she could somehow walk out of and away from herself when her shyness made her very soul shake, like now.

It was time to get ready for her lunch date with Ralph. Her breath was suddenly coming harder.

$\triangledown$

4

As NINA'S TAXI sped along FDR Drive, the river was a vat of blue molten metal, light rising in sparks from its surface. How could her meeting with Ralph be anything but terrific on such a day?

Chauncy's was precisely the kind of romantic restaurant she had hoped Ralph would choose. The dining room was a great grotto full of the glint and gleam of precious things. Sunlight coming through a skylight made the mahogany bar shine like tarnished gold. Linen blinded her. Glassware chimed. Everywhere there was the scent of lemons.

She was fifteen minutes early. Although she seldom drank, she ordered a glass of valpolicella so Ralph wouldn't think she was a prude. Nervous, she went into the women's room to examine her appearance. She had washed her hair twice but as usual it hadn't responded. She had dressed and undressed four times before putting on a floral print dress with a lace collar.

He was late. While she waited time was split in two. There was ordinary time, measurable by her watch. Then there was the fiery rush inside her head, as if the mainspring had sprung and all the movements were spinning out of control.

She grew lightheaded from the wine, volatile. The floor beneath her was stretched tight as a trampoline.

But when Ralph finally arrived, nineteen minutes late, she couldn't stop feeling hopeful. True, he had a raw, jagged look to him, as if he had been exposed for a long time to some far rougher form of weather than she knew. And he spoke quickly, like a man accustomed to pushing through obstacles. His voice was guttural, yet impressive—even seductive in an odd way.

He extended his hand warily, as if she might keep it. Did his look also contain disapproval, or was that just her imagination?

But those eyes of his—like delphinium long steeped in water. And that hair—like wet black paint.

With a cigarette dangling from a corner of his mouth, one eye screwed shut against the smoke, Ralph ordered something called "Dewar's rocks."

As he gulped his drink, the silence rose around her like water.

"So what do you think?" he finally said.

Think about what? Him? His choice of restaurant? Their first meeting? Why was she always so terrible at these things? All her life she had observed girls and women to whom it came so smoothly and easily.

She tried to speak and discovered that her tongue was dry and swollen.

"What do you mean?" she finally said, hating her response. Hating her knees for shaking under the table.

The silence tightened and tightened, like something being twisted closed.

She began to have the familiar feeling that she was utterly unlike herself. She knew she was sitting next to Ralph, who was fretfully twiddling his thumbs, yet simultaneously she—the real, businesslike, assertive her—had gotten herself trapped inside a body not her own.

"Got to go to the john," he said, startling her.

As he rose she bolted the rest of her wine, though she knew how disoriented drinking would make her.

When he didn't return in eleven minutes the idea that he never would made the very heart of things stop. After sixteen minutes the air itself seemed damaged. At twenty minutes she felt as though she had been struck down.

The waiter stopped by. She ordered another drink, trying to appear unconcerned.

As more time passed she felt like an empty bottle that was slowly being filled with cold, filthy water.

Suddenly she had a vivid sense of herself: something pallid and slack. She became aware of her toenails, her anus, her damp, constricted crotch. She avoided the waiter's eyes. The air had become thick. The seats gave off a sat-upon smell.

After Ralph had been gone over thirty minutes, she took his last letter to her from her purse. She read it for the same reason that a dog bites a wound—to hurt the pain.

When one side of her head began to throb, Nina blamed it on Ralph. But then she felt a familiar extreme sensitivity to noise. The sound of a page turning on a menu plucked at her nerves. Then the muted yellow light from the room's lamps blinded her. Pain struck her so hard behind the right eye that she had to grab the table. The eye began to tear. Nausea rose.

She held onto the table, shaking, dreading the dark unknown.

When the pain became unbearable, Nina threw some bills down on the table and went home. She would lie on her bed in the dark, try to exorcise the hammering in her head.

The instant she entered the bedroom her eyes went blank, then closed. She stood rigid, lids fluttering. A slight shudder passed over her entire body. Then her eyes blinked open, looking distant, as if turned inward. Her lips twitched, as they did when she mumbled in her sleep.

Suddenly, as though she had awakened from sleep in a cramped position, her body began to shift and expand, carrying out innumerable, barely discernible adjustments.

A pair of defiant, mischievous eyes now appeared, their pupils dilated, giving them a darker hue. The shape of her body seemed voluptuous and feline now. Her thin-lipped mouth had a new fullness and contour. The small involuntary movements and nuances through which her usual poses and expressions reflected her personality were markedly

different. The sometimes shy businesswoman had become
a lush, provocative female with a look of brash vitality and
the essence of debauchery.

She called herself Carmina Rivincita.

She had never once had a headache.

▽

5

"MAY WE ALL live to be a hundred, with one extra year to repent," said Nora Cassidy.

She clicked glasses with Casey, Kate, and Josh. Then she gave Casey a big kiss.

Kate and Josh looked on delightedly. It had been a long time since they'd seen the New York City's chief of detectives so happy. Gone was the bruised expression his gnarled face had held since his wife's death six years ago. His sad, washed-out blue eyes had become glittering lapis lazuli. Even his gray hair with its cowlick now had the gleam of aluminum.

"What's this stuff we're drinking, anyway?" Casey said. He had a voice like a yard rake on slate.

Josh said, "Bermuda black rum with ginger beer. Here it's called a Dark and Stormy."

"Where I come from," Casey said, "it's called sweet and sticky."

"Don't talk dirty," Nora said.

All four burst out laughing.

Kate studied Nora. She was a big-boned, earthy, middle-aged woman with blunt features and a throaty voice. Her frequent gestures were grand and uncontrolled. Her eyes were huge and perfectly oval and had the sheen of dark, wet mahogany. Kate thought she had never seen prettier eyes, or ones so full of undiminished optimism.

Donelle brought steaming plates of food.

All agreed the meal—grouper chowder, mussel pie with stewed tomatoes and onion sauce—was delicious.

Afterward, Casey took Josh aside. The two old friends were soon walking barefoot on the beach.

"I have to tell somebody," Casey said, "or bust. Sixty-three years old, feel like a kid. No, never felt this young."

"Never seen you look this good. Kate and me, we're very happy for you. Nora's so real. Not afraid to be herself. A mensch."

"And what a rip. I think of Moira, rest in peace, and I know there'll continue to be a small piece torn out of every day for the rest of my life. After she was gone there were a few women. But it was like trying to jump-start my car and the motor wouldn't catch. Being a cop you meet all kinds. Some women need you to wear the whole rig to bed, piece and all, or they can't get off. . . . You know I never believed in locker room talk, but I need to tell you . . . Nora and me, we take baths. Together. Can you believe it?"

"Sure I can." Josh smiled

Casey thought of how fortunate he had been with women. First Moira, now Nora. Last night after he had come, Nora said, smiling, "Wait a minute," and kissed his eyes. Then she gazed at him till he felt as if she were lowering herself into his very soul.

He had sweated with pleasure, feeling the perspiration flow like mercury out through his pores, freeing him. He felt she was pulling his blood back downward with her smile, down from his head and heart and stomach to engorge his penis. Afterward, swallowing him and then drying him with her hair.

"Casey?"

The detective looked around. "Sorry. Anyway . . ." He started to tell Josh about the way they sometimes spoke to each other on the phone, but decided not to. How he liked sleeping in the same bed, drinking coffee poured from the same pot in the mornings. "I was dead for so long after Moira . . . now I got a new chance. Thinking differently about the job, too."

"How's that?"

"Last week a judge gave one of my men a search warrant that was declared invalid. The detective was held responsible without pay, 'cause a judge can't be wrong."

"That kind of thing's nothing new."

"But it's worse. Damn Internal Affairs is always after my people. Cops used to take care of their own."

Casey stopped walking, and both men sat on the coral sand looking out at the phosphorescent blackness of the ocean in the bright moonlight.

"Stress," Casey said. "It used to be called nerves. Then it was nervous breakdowns. Remember? Now it's stress. Burnout. All in the head."

"Always was." Josh saw that Casey's blue eyes had suddenly become so washed-out that they appeared iron-colored. He noticed the ruddiness of the Chief's nose, the hundreds of burst capillaries of a heavy drinker.

"Thinking of quitting, Josh. Maybe find a nice place in the country like you and Kate have in Rhinebeck. Look the seasons in the eye."

For an instant his gnarled face was a boy's. Then the boy was gone, and a man in difficulty sat next to Josh. A man who looked as if gravity were crushing him.

"But this new case," Casey went on, "is driving me crazy, like I said. Have to solve it before I hang it up. We got nothing. No prints, no blood, not a single hair or thread. Just the same MO."

"What about the victims?"

"One's twenty-eight, one's thirty-five, and another's forty-three. One owned a pet shop, one was a high school teacher, and another was a computer salesman. The salesman was Irish, the pet shop guy was Italian, the teacher was Hispanic. Like that. All three had come minutes before they were killed."

"Charming. You said all three murders happened in hotels. Anybody see the victims with somebody?"

"One guy was seen with a brunette, another with a

redhead. And then a blond. Got to be the same killer, though. Same MO. Probably a gay one in drag. You got any idea how many women a New York hotel bartender sees in just one night? Caught a break, though—bartenders in all three places knew exactly who my detectives were asking about, right away."

"Why? Weird looking?"

"A movie star. A *fageleh* that gorgeous could kill practically every guy in the city, he has the time."

"Speaking of time—"

"Yeah, we better get back."

"Then maybe you can explain why the three murders have the same MO. I don't see where they're connected."

▽

6

Rᴀʟᴘʜ Wᴇɪʀ ꜱᴘʟᴀꜱʜᴇᴅ musk cologne on his face and then sprayed deodorant under his arms again. He moved frenetically: speed soothed him.

Through the open bathroom window the early evening gray sky looked as if it had been rubbed with a soiled dustcloth. Only an idiot would let weather influence his moods. Especially today, when using the personals ads to score promised to pay off bigger than ever. Take the taste out of his mouth from that lame nun Nina Benanti with her librarian's dress. Jesus, what a waste.

This one's letter had sounded hot, and it'd been her idea to come to his place. "See where you live, cutie," she'd said. He'd show her *live*.

He hurried through the apartment making a last-minute check. Dimmed the lights in the bedroom and smoothed out the satin sheets. Looking in one of the strategically placed mirrors, he smiled at his reflection. Pretty fucking good for a fifty-one-year-old dude. And not one gray hair showed through the recent dye job.

He inventoried the drawer of the nightstand: sheer condoms, vibrator, K-Y jelly. Never knew how lucky he'd get.

In the living room he programmed the CD player so that the music would gradually progress from romantic ballads to sensual instrumentals.

When the doorman buzzed to say he had a woman guest, Ralph hurried to fill the ice bucket. At the sound of the bell he spritzed his mouth twice with an aerosol breath spray and opened the door.

"Well," she said, laughing, "are you going to serve drinks in the hall?"

The blond who leaned suggestively against his doorpost wore a scant white top and black Spandex pants. She had the face of a model and the body of an aerobics instructor. He felt the blood moving to his groin.

There was something challenging in her snotty laughter. But he put this aside, delighted at his incredible luck.

"Come in, please," he said, hearing the excitement in his voice.

She looked back at him with a kind of impersonal intensity. He flinched as if suddenly caught in a strong light. No one had ever looked at him quite like that before. He felt he should be indignant or at least play at being so, but the usual responses did not seem to be appropriate with her. Besides, he couldn't resist her partial nudity. His fingers could sense the silkiness and weight and density, the glimmering patina, of the flesh of her bare midriff. His clothes felt tight as bandages.

"Are you going to offer me a drink or not, Ralphie?"

At the portable bar in the living room the ice turned treacherous, slithering off his hands.

Seeing her sitting on his imitation leopard-skin bar-stool, legs spread apart, he felt a growing weight in his groin. He pictured her naked lap sprawled and open as halved fruit. How he'd love to find and press a secret nerve in her so that she would turn to him with a groan and cling to him as if she were falling. To change the spark of insistent teasing in her eyes to hunger and defenselessness. Have her flinch under the delicious damage he inflicted on her.

"Is Ralphie nervous?" she said, tossing her hair like a

surfaced swimmer. "Why don't you come here and give me a real hello?"

He went, feeling strangely that it was he who was slowly, irresistibly, being penetrated.

She kissed him gently on his mouth. Then buried her triangular face like the blade of an ax in his neck.

"Carmina," he groaned.

▽

7

"So what makes you so sure these three heart attack victims were murdered?" Kate said to Casey as the four of them drank coffee and ate rum-soaked sponge cake with jam and cherry sauce.

"None of the guys had a heart condition, so why would they be taking digitalis?"

Josh said, "I don't understand. Of all the male heart attack victims in New York City in just *one day*, let alone on three separate days, how did you put these three men together?"

"All three had an overdose of digitalis. All three had twenty-dollar bills folded like handkerchiefs in the lapel pockets of their jackets. I had my people checking the computer bank for other murders with the digitalis and the twenties. They'll keep at it."

"Couldn't they have put the bills there to pay hookers?" Kate said.

"Hookers don't go to fancy hotel rooms looking to score only twenty dollars. Something more's going on."

"Like?" Kate said.

Casey put his hands together over his head and grimaced, pulling down an imaginary weight. "Like maybe some gay serial killer in drag, or a transvestite."

"Why not a woman serial killer?" Nora said.

"No such animal," Casey said. He set his fork down. "According to the FBI there's never been one."

"Since when," Kate said, "do you always agree with the

FBI? What do you call that prostitute who killed eight men in Florida a few years ago?"

Casey pushed his plate away. "FBI says when women do kill they tend to choose people they know."

Kate stood and began pacing. "Look, the FBI is a bunch of men making definitions. If they said people have to stand to urinate, would you say women don't pee?

"Listen, Case, Sir Arthur Conan Doyle even came up with a Jill-the-Ripper theory. Doyle lived in London at the time, and he figured only a woman could move around Whitechapel that way without arousing suspicion. They even had a 'Jill the Ripper' song going around London after that."

Casey said, "Why are you so sure it's a woman?"

"I'm just saying it could be. It bothers me that you're being so closed-minded."

"So," Casey said, rising and pouring Kate and the others a brandy, "my absolute last case before I hang it up."

"Are you serious?" Nora beamed.

"Damn right." He turned to Kate and Josh. "Will you two help me?"

"On one condition, as far as I'm concerned . . ." Kate said, looking at Josh.

Josh nodded.

"Name it," Casey said.

Kate said, "You agree to listen to what our family doctor here told you about getting your drinking below world-class level."

"What's 'below world-class level'?"

Josh said, "Two ounces of whiskey a day."

"That's blackmail," Casey said. He looked at the ceiling. Then shook his head. "All right, when do we start?"

"Right now," said Nora. "Put down that brandy. You've already had your quota."

▽

8

JOSH WAS READING Kate a letter that Casey had FedExed: "Anyway, this playboy Weir, the victim, turns out to be married with three bambinos. Our murderer stuck the usual twenty in his lapel pocket after blowing his heart apart."

"So far all the victims were married with kids. You think—"

"I think—I *know*—I'm going to tell Donelle to hold any mail till we're ready to leave. And I'm not going to open it till we're back home. We have three more days and I'm going to enjoy every second of them. Okay with you?"

"Dandy with me. More wine?"

He poured them each a glassful.

They sat on the porch letting the silence stretch for a time. The ocean was a great blue satin dress sequined by the sun. Josh leaned over, kissed her on the forehead, and stroked her cheek.

She looked into his face and saw his familiarly comforting patience with her mood. "You know I love that son of a bitch. But sometimes he's the most inconsiderate bastard—he knows we only have seventy-two hours left, but—"

"You're absolutely right."

"Go on. You may as well finish it."

" 'Naturally, darlin', I don't want to bother you two on vacation, but I hoped I could just get this new information into your mental computers as soon as possible.' Cute."

Kate slammed down her drink so hard some of it flew out of her glass. "You buy that shit?"

"No."

"Doesn't want to bother us on vacation! Who does he think he's fooling."

It wasn't a question.

"Not us," Josh said.

She turned quickly toward him, as though she were the Pope and he had suggested Mother Teresa was streetwalking on the side. "You like teasing me, huh?" She was losing her battle to keep from smiling. "Stop laughing or I swear I'll stick this croissant in your tush."

"I love when you talk that way."

She bit her lip to stop the smile, but he had already seen it.

"But I *am* pissed at him, all right?"

"Perfectly all right."

"You patronize me one more—*damn*." She gave a sudden raucous laugh. "I hate you. I mean I *really* hate you."

"Maybe that explains our compatibility—mutual abhorrence. What else is gnawing at you?" he said, pouring them each a little of what remained of the wine.

She thought about all that he liked about living in the country: the fresh air, the clear skies for his sky watching, the quiet . . . "You won't like it," she said.

"Please."

"Rhinebeck. Not the town. The people. Since we moved from the city neither one of us has made a single friend. The dogs say hello to us in town. We've got an army of acquaintances. But not one friend."

"I know. Go on, honey."

"I know how you love that place, but unless you were born there you'll always be considered a stranger. And that's another thing. They've got us down as being strange. I don't like that."

"Since when do you care what people think?"

"Since I need friends. Oh Josh, a couple of times when I slept at a hotel in the city when I was working with Case I actually heard rumors when I came home."

"Not really."

"Yes."

"Please go on."

"I can hear them thinking, 'What kind of woman special-
izes in sex crimes? What kind of man chooses to cut up dead
people?' When I go to the Grand Union people actually stare
to see what we eat, how we live."

He reached over and took her into his arms. "I don't think
I want to move back to the city," he said evenly, "but I'm
certainly open to talk about it."

"God, I love you. I don't want to go back to the city either.
It's even more dangerous and dirty, and noisier than ever.
The worst for me is it's lost so much of its ethnicity. So many
of the new immigrants—Koreans, Russians, Israelis—don't
want any part of a melting pot."

He downed the dregs from his glass. "For me it's the loss
of the middle class who can no longer afford it. Only the rich
and the poor remain."

She passed him her glass. He put up his palm in protest.

"Please," he said, "I'm done."

She said, "Not to mention that the median age there
now seems to be twenty-five. People look at me like I'm
late for a henna rinse."

"Not hardly. But I know what you mean. Let me tell you
that I do love the country, but there's a lot of country besides
Rhinebeck. And if you're not happy in a place then I don't
want to be there."

"God, you're an inconsiderate bastard."

"One of the worst. And for a criminologist you're some
detective. Casey's case and how you're feeling about
Rhinebeck—they're connected, you know. The case may
mean your sleeping over in the city again, which will bring
the local suspicions again. No doubt our faces will be in the
papers and—"

"And a lot of the locals'll think we help Casey so we can
be in the limelight."

She slapped herself in the forehead and said, "Great
Caesar's ghost!" mimicking Clark Kent's boss Perry White.

"Don't be such a wise guy or you may find yourself part of the legion of women whose husbands went out for a pack of cigarettes and never came home."

"You don't smoke."

"So I'll start. I've seen some locals look at me the way you said. You don't have to live with that bullshit. Where do you want to move to?"

"I don't know. One thing at a time."

"You keep up that kind of talk you'll soon have a reputation as a sage."

"*Funny.*"

She looked out toward the Bermudian horizon as though she knew it would be the last she would see of it in a long time. In the watery light the sea was a pan of enameled water.

She said, "I'm going into town to phone that relentless cop masquerading as our friend."

"You're that mad at him?"

"No. I thought of something he may not have thought of."

$\triangledown$

9

"As God is my witness, Kate," Casey said into the phone receiver, "all I wanted was to get the new information to you and Josh. Didn't mean to spoil Bermuda for you."

"If God is your witness then you've got an even more spectacular gift for blarney than I thought. What's that I hear you swallowing?"

"Station-house coffee. Now is that any way to speak to a man who's been a good friend to you, your husband, and your dear father, man and cop?"

"Hold on Case."

"What is it?"

"I just wanted to get my harp to accompany you."

This time her humor didn't escape him, and he laughed loudly.

"What's going on in that fine head of yours?" he said. "Or is it Josh's *kepeleh* this idea came out of?"

"Before we even get to that—"

"Now, you're not going to treat me like a red-cheeked little boy, Katie, and ask the number of whiskeys I've had today?"

"No. I'm going to treat you like a red-nosed big man and ask the number of *ounces* you had today."

"Not a one yet."

"What do you mean, 'yet'? Bermuda is one hour ahead of New York, which makes it six twenty-one. What happened to your happy hour?"

"I'm waiting to share with my Nora the generous ration you and your anti-Celt husband blackmailed me into promising. You'd never get away with this in Holy Ireland."

"How is Nora?"

"Even more determined to deny me an extra dab of the brush than you. Other than that she's a—they don't make 'em better, darlin'."

"Say hello, will you?"

"And the same to Josh. Now on with it please. You don't want to make me frustrated as well as thirsty."

"You mean you know the difference?"

"Katie—"

"All right. Did Forensics find any pubic hairs?"

"Now you're telling me you think I'm that bad a detective I didn't pick up that stone?"

"You're a wonderful detective."

"I agree. Besides, you know it's very hard to tell race or even sex from short and curlies—excuse me—pubes, except if you got a Caucasian or black or—"

"So that's what the boys in blue call them—charming, as Josh would say."

"Something's not right here. You didn't call me from Bermuda to check on pubic hairs."

"Yes, I did. Were there any?"

"Not a one in any of the cases."

"Aha."

"Aha what?"

"Aha it's too early to say yet."

"Say it anyway. I won't tell if you're wrong."

"You know I don't believe—"

"In talking away a hunch. Yes. I should know by now. What else?"

"Nothing else. Was there any deviation from the pattern here? At all?"

"None. We thought there was till we found out Weir was married with kids too. The digitalis, the folded twenty, everything. Cookie cutter."

When she didn't say anything he said, "Hey, c'mon, give. I can smell good Irish wood burning from here."

"That's your thirst smoking."

"Speaking of which, that's all I've gotten from this conversation."

"I said you're a wonderful detective," Kate said. "That's not the same as the best. I got to go, really."

"What have you got in mind to torture me with tomorrow?"

"Oh, that'll arrive FedEx by ten-thirty A.M."

"*Really?* What is it?"

"An eight-by-ten glossy of a quart of J.J. and S. twelve-year-old."

"Now I know what kind of sadistic woman you really are."

"Now you know."

"Christ sakes. To solve a case you need means and motive and opportunity. I don't have a one. I wish I was Columbo."

"Careful what you're praying for. Nora hates cigars."

There was a stretch of silence. Kate imagined him staring into his coffee cup the way she'd seen him stare into a glass of whiskey. For one night at least, she wished she could give him his fill of J.J. and S. to soften the pouty mouth she knew he now wore.

"Good night, you handsome black Irish devil."

"And to you, you witch."

"Kidding aside. How's it going with the sauce?"

"There are easier things than two ounces a day. I just don't know any. But I was drinking with both hands. I love and hate you all for doing this."

"Understand."

"We got another monster here, don't we, Kate?"

"It's not Francis of Assisi killing these guys."

"All I want is to be there to take him—it—down."

"You usually are."

"No. What I'm saying, *me,* not someone else."

"I never saw you take a case this personally before."

"I never handed in my shield before."

10

Nina froze when she turned on the TV for the six o'clock news and heard: "A police spokesman has confirmed that the death last night of Manhattan food broker Ralph Weir appears to be the latest in a series of murders in which heart attacks were induced by digitalis. Weir, the fourth victim, is survived by a wife and three children. For more details watch the seven o'clock report."

She began to shake with shock. "I was just sitting across a table from him, and now he's dead." Then anger made the roots of her teeth ache. "Married—with three children—"

After a time anger shifted to hurt, and she began to cry silently. Then in great racking sobs.

As the cries finally subsided, a memory invaded her mind. She saw herself at age six being led through a part of the city with buildings so tall it made her dizzy to look up at them. A big hand held her own. She saw that it was her father's hand. Poppa stopped in front of a house little Nina recognized, and she smiled, thinking of all the fun she'd have there.

Now a great terror seized Nina, punching the air from her lungs. Her memory emptied as if a plug were pulled.

She stood quickly in an effort to speed the present back into herself. "The panic comes from losing Poppa," she told herself. And stomped into the kitchen, where she put on the kettle for some soothing chamomile tea.

While she waited to hear the kettle whistle, she went and sat before the saltwater aquarium in the library. She turned on the aquarium light and watched as her pearlfish, which she knew had spent the night feeding on microscopic food, sought out a sea cucumber.

Slowly, Nina's thoughts turned from her horrible morning, and most of her attention focused on the pearlfish. Tail first, it entered the sea cucumber as it opened its anus to "breathe" by drawing water through its respiratory system. She watched as the pearlfish squirmed deeper into the sea cucumber, where it would rest for the day, reversing the process when she switched off the light.

Sometimes when the pain became too great she wished that she, too, could crawl into someone's life, safe from the responsibility of her own decisions.

Then she doggedly made herself do some of the things she knew would lift her spirits.

She watered the plants in the window. Few things were more uplifting than giving flowers a drink. Then she put seed in the bird feeder. How full of wings the air in the backyard was when Poppa was alive and always bringing the birds new treats!

The chamomile comforted her and brought to mind the many afternoons she and her father had lain on the chaise longue in the backyard, sipping tea and eating cannoli. The memory knitted what the horrible morning had unraveled in her.

After a breakfast of strawberries in oatmeal she found where she'd left off in May Sarton's latest book, *Endgame*. How she wished she had the woman's courage. How she wished she were whole again as when her father—her *parents*, she corrected herself, ashamed—were alive. How she wished she had not been so tethered to them.

She rose and fed the fishes in all six aquariums. She took particular delight watching four-day-old angelfish eating newly hatched brine shrimp. Earlier she had fed the shrimp liquid vitamins and minerals through an eyedropper—a technique her father had taught her, to raise hardier angels.

She considered phoning her friend Cynthia, but she didn't

want to press her loneliness on anyone else. After all, who was without loneliness and pain?

Instead she changed the water in a vase containing a delicate pale pink orchid that looked to her like the joined wings of several butterflies.

It wasn't loneliness for a single or a specific person, but a feeling that she couldn't handle the pain. How different life had turned out from what she had once taken for granted. Where were her children? Her husband?

What was it Poppa had always said? "Expect a miracle!" But for too long she had lost her ability to do that.

Thoughts of Ralph Weir returned, but she crushed them and sat for a while looking at the quality of the changing light through the leaves. She would go to the florist and buy some anemones. She loved to watch them open wide, showing their purple hearts at the center. And maybe some white freesias too. What white in the world compared with that?

She saw her father's face then. What beauty was there. The way feeling crossed it like the gentle lap of a lake sometimes, when a smile began there or an accepting look of pain.

Nina wrenched herself from this thought that made her heart so heavy it ached.

When a cardinal flew into the feeder, its wings alight, she opened Sarton's book.

She was again amazed at the woman's ability to go on. As she read, it seemed she would never have to step back into her own life.

▽

11

KATE STUDIED THE detectives as they began to fill the briefing room. A smell of rain and wet wool and tiredness came off them. In their faces she saw the fatigue of working on a case with too few clues. A few smiled. Some, whose faces she didn't recognize, looked at her with wariness, even contempt, as if to say they knew more about serial murderers than someone who had learned about them in books.

Casey stood next to her and the lone window in the room, on which rain ticked. Weariness was evident in his blue eyes, so pale they scarcely showed in his face. His skin was stretched over the bones. He had lost some weight after cutting down his drinking, and his once-florid corpulence had diminished like a slowly leaking balloon. Humidity and lack of grooming made his hair, which usually had the gleam of aluminum, look like a crinkled gray fern.

"All right," Casey began. "Most of you know that Dr. Berman here is no desk criminologist. For those of you who are new and didn't read the papers much the last few years, this is the same Kate Berman who found the Lauren Bacall Killer. Before that she almost bought it catching the Central Park Slasher."

An old fear made Kate feel as if the floor beneath her had suddenly fallen away.

"—so listen up now to Dr. Berman."

The applause had always been embarrassing—even now,

as she remembered the Slasher's blade entering her and that strange flowerlike stain like a melted red anemone spreading in the waist of her dress.

When she had made her way to the front of the room and found her voice, she said, "I'm not here because I profess to know one percent of what any of you know about crime on the streets. But I do know something about serial killers. Please interrupt, ask questions. This is no lecture."

She took a drink of water from the aluminum carafe Casey had provided on the small dais.

"This year so far there have been eighteen thousand five hundred and twelve murders in America classified as 'without motive'—homicide without reward of any kind except the killing itself. For these crimes, twenty-one suspects have been captured. Eight have been convicted. This does not include another four to six thousand corpses that show up unidentified. So I'm being conservative here."

Kate looked around the room. She had gotten their attention.

" 'Without motive' murders are perpetrated by one of two different types of killers. The first is mentally ill, like the character Anthony Perkins played in *Psycho*.

"The second—and there're many more of them—is your recreational killer or rake. These are considered sane. Bundy, Gacey, Dahmer."

Delighted to see notebooks suddenly popping open, she paused.

"Rakes are not insane but are born without emotions. We also call them 'devoids.' "

More notebooks appeared.

"Explaining feelings to them would be like interpreting music to a deaf person."

"So is that how we recognize a devoid?" a woman detective Kate knew as Kelsey said.

"Yes and no, detective."

The room burst into noisy whisperings.

"Devoids, as a rule, have much higher intelligence than

most of us. They *know* that they don't have the capacity to feel and are different from us. If you're in a movie theater with them, they'll watch to see when to laugh or cry. Some law enforcement agents have begun calling them 'parrots.' "

Notebooks appeared like a flotilla of black-and-white butterflies. Kate had found that new buzzwords never failed to hold the attention of police professionals.

"So how do we recognize them?" an Asian detective called out.

"It's the time they need to take watching us *before* they begin to parrot that gives them away, Zhang."

"Problem is," said a young detective Kate didn't recognize, "how do you even begin to suspect one of them? We know now most of these guys aren't living under bridges like trolls. They're sitting next to us at Little League or PTA. Our kids play with their kids."

"That's very true detective, uh—?"

"Oulton."

"Detective Oulton, if you're part of the average family the chances are better than one in three that you'll meet a devoid."

The room exploded into talk.

Casey called: "What is this—a freaking Welcome Wagon klatch?"

The noise abated.

"So what's the answer?" Oulton continued. "How do we find these guys?"

"Devoids are not exactly limited to males," Kate said.

"Anybody ever met my first wife could tell you that," shouted a black detective.

The room erupted with laughter. Kate couldn't help chuckling.

"All right, all right," Casey implored. But he was smiling himself.

"We—you—find these people with good old-fashioned police work. Routine."

"Specifically?" Kelsey said.

"Specifically forensics. Especially microforensics. Specifically profiling."

"You mean," Kelsey went on, "like if a killer covers a victim it means he has a little regret or guilt?"

"No, because devoids—"

"Yes, I forgot. They don't feel regret or guilt. So what do we look for—things like strangulation showing a disorganized personality?"

"Exactly! Which is certainly not what we're dealing with here." She saw Casey signaling her that her time was coming to an end. "Which is what our next talk will be about."

The officers began to rise.

"You haven't been dismissed yet," Casey yelled.

Those standing sat.

"By the way, Detective Oulton," Kate said, "your use of the word 'troll' earlier was most fortunate."

"How's that, doctor?"

"Sexual killers nowadays call stalking their victims 'wilding' or 'trolling.' "

The notebooks reappeared.

"Now," Kate said after she and Casey were back in his office, "would you explain why you cut my time when I was just getting to the most important stuff?"

Casey stood from behind his desk and walked over to the window.

"Well—" he began.

"Well, nothing. Before you start to manipulate me again, tell me you didn't do it to make sure I had to come back to finish. Keep their interest piqued for another week."

"Well—"

"Well, huh? Well, let me tell you something, Mr. Chief of Detectives—there's nothing I hate more than being manipulated."

"I'm sorry, Katie. I'm desperate. This case went from me holding off from the papers on the first two murders to this Weir guy now becoming front-page. Even a nickname for the killer."

" 'Widowmaker.' Charming."

"You sound like Josh. How is he?"

"Sweet Jesus. Do I look that dumb you could get away with switching subjects that easy?"

"You're anything but an easy County Sligo woman."

"And there's no need to remind me our parents came from the same place. And stop looking at me with those blue beagle eyes of yours."

"Could you find it in your heart to speak to my detectives again at your convenience?"

" 'Could I find it in my heart' says he. Give it a rest, Case."

"Is that a yes?"

"It's not a no."

$\bigtriangledown$

12

"Katie? It's me, Case. He—or whatever—did another one."

"Where are you?"

"My car. On the way to the scene. I thought maybe you'd want to see things fresh this time."

"You thought right."

"Ninety Lexington, between twenty-sixth and twenty-seventh. Apartment Seven-M. I could send a chopper to Rhinebeck. You just say the word."

"That'd save a lot of time. Yes. Thanks."

"I was thinking, maybe Josh—you know he's still the best in the world, forensically speaking—maybe he might see something my people missed."

"Hold on." She kept the receiver close to her mouth and shouted: "Honey, Case wants to know if you can find it in your heart to come to a crime scene with me." Pause. "No problem, Case."

"You're a wicked woman poking fun at a man just trying to do his job."

"See you in an hour then. Chins up, Case."

"You keep holding back my whiskey, I'll soon have only one like everyone else. The chopper's already on its way."

When Kate and Josh arrived, the smell was like opening a can of cat food with your nose too close to it. Casey, as if to compensate for his whiskey having been rationed, had gone back to Camels. He stood next to two gold shields Kate remembered from the briefing, drawing in smoke as though it were life-extending.

"Sorry," he said to Kate, "I already told them to open the windows and spill ammonia."

As Kate and Josh examined the body, one CSU man's strobe lit up the bedroom theatrically while he took still shots of the body from all angles with a Nikon. A CSU woman with a retractable tape was taking measurements of the body's distance from nearby walls and furniture and making notes on a sketch she'd made of the scene.

Kate studied the handsome, thirtyish dead man who lay on the floor, then looked up at Josh, who said, "Could be a heart attack. But we'll have to wait for the autopsy to see if it was too much digitalis. He'd been drinking. That's for sure."

She went over to the CSU man, who was examining the rumpled bed, where a pair of men's pants, dress shirt, tie, and sports jacket hung from one of the four posts.

The CSU man who had been taking photographs was now dusting for fingerprints with the white powder used exclusively by the NYPD. He pressed transparent tape to the ones he chose, lifted them, and transferred them to dark-colored backing paper.

"Anybody check the traps in the tub and sink?" she heard Casey say.

One of the gold shields took a clear plastic evidence bag from the CSU kit and disappeared into the bathroom. Kate guessed there just might be some hairs in the drains that could lead to this killer.

She saw that in the victim's lapel pocket there was a twenty-dollar bill, folded identically to the bills found with the other victims.

When the medical examiner arrived, Kate shook his hand, left Josh with him, and continued to study the scene. Both hands were clasped peacefully over the victim's chest. The hair was neatly three-quarter parted and looked as though it had been finger-combed. A towel was draped over his middle, covering his sex. When she looked closely, she saw fresh scratch marks on the right side of the neck. The uniforms in the hall, who had been trying to control the expanding knot of curious tenants who might contaminate the crime scene, were being hard pressed. A young Asian assistant district attorney plus reporters and photographers from the *Post* and the *News*, a camera crew from Channel Seven, and six more detectives had all arrived. The newspeople were unhappy about having to wait outside.

When Kate returned to Josh, he had joined Casey, who was talking to the gold shields.

"Break up into two-man teams. Start with the tenants in the hall and check the building from top to bottom. I want anyone and everyone who knew the deceased all questioned."

"So?" Casey said to Kate and Josh as they sat at a table in a bar called Gillogly's.

"So," Josh said, "between seven and eight hours old. The scratches have a trailer at the ends like a little tail. Scratches like that are typically made by a left-handed person."

"What do you say, Katie?" Casey asked, downing half his day's ration of whiskey.

"I say you know that killers who disfigure their victims' faces tend to know them at least reasonably well. And neck wounds are characteristic of gay homicides. That, plus the fact that killers who spend a lot of time at the crime scene usually live nearby, as this one obviously does—"

"Means," Casey said, "I should be looking for a fruit that's a southpaw who lives nearby and knew the victim pretty well."

"Give that man a silver dollar," Kate said.

"You're not telling me I'm holding an invitation to the Pope's wedding, are you, Katie?"

"I'm afraid so, Case. This one's a copycat."

When Casey was able to speak, he ordered his final whiskey of the day.

▽

13

NINA HAD ALREADY locked her office door and was turning to leave when she was startled by Milt Furman. The Widowmaker murders were making her more nervous than usual.

"Sorry, Nina." His words were like barrels rumbling in a basement. "Were you leaving?"

"What gave you the first clue?" She saw that he was troubled and gently added, "Never closed for you."

Breathless delight arose in the exhausted face, especially in his oyster-colored eyes. There were scores of scratchy lines of shadow under his eyes and a redness surrounding the rims she had never seen before. His complexion, normally that of a baker at work, now looked bleached. His mouth was full but bloodless. The look of experience and good sense that had been in his eyes the many years that she'd known him had been replaced by the wistful expression of a dog trying to understand.

She remembered her father's delight watching a pair of Milt's discus fish performing their mating dance. She was grateful to Milt for keeping the memory alive and green. It was balm to her.

"What's inside that bag?" she said, opening the office.

In his odd, studied way, as if there were sweetness in his silence, he withdrew a plastic bag from within the brown paper one. Then something very close to a smile appeared on his lips as he took a penlight from a pocket of his baggy pants and shone it on the fish.

She approached the bag. "Since when do you carry fish into my office?"

"Since I want you to see the pinnacle of the breeder's art."

Milt was the sole distributor for Tso Churk Yinn, a famous Hong Kong breeder of discus. She made note that he had not mentioned Tso's name specifically.

"Beautiful," Nina said. "I never saw an orange discus. And look at that black dusting on the dorsal! Is this a new strain of Tso's?"

"A new strain, yes."

"How much?"

"Twelve dollars in dozen lots. Ten a hundred if I can have the money with the order."

"That's fair. Would you like some iced tea or juice? You look tired."

"Yes, I am. Tea would be nice. Thanks."

After she'd handed him a glass of iced tea from the miniature refrigerator she could hear him swallowing.

"Thanks," he said. "How many do you want?"

"To start I'll take the dozen you got in the bag."

His face suddenly emptied of all expression except fear.

"No, no, not these. I can't sell you these. They're not for sale. But in four weeks I can have as many as you want."

"Sit down Milt. Please." She gently directed him into a chair. "I've known you a long time. You've always been honest and dependable. A pleasure to do business with."

"A pleasure," he said as if it were an "amen."

"But now you're not telling me the truth. You're lying by omission. These are not Tso's fish. But you never told me they were. You won't sell me this bag of fish not because they're promised to someone or you need them to show buyers—you always use photographs. You know what I think?"

Milt remained silent.

"I think you bought these fish from someone like Duong in Singapore. They looked in perfect health so you didn't quarantine them. But they were carriers of something. Your fish room came down with the disease. You wouldn't sell me these fish because you're too honest. But you're broke and you need money, and you know I always give you your money up front."

She could feel Milt sinking down inside himself, growing heavy in his stillness, vague in his thoughts. When he looked up it was excruciating to witness his grief.

"I—I'm sorry. I never once lied to you before. I'm desperate. Last year my younger son—you know the one—talked Thelma and me out of our last penny in the bank for some cockamamy franchise you shouldn't know from. Poof. Gone. All the money. Then that *gonif* Duong—his head should grow in the ground like an onion—destroyed my whole fish room with these." He raised the bag. "I'm ruined."

"Not quite. You never really lied to me or this conversation wouldn't be happening. Neither would it if you had sold me these particular fish. How many fish did you lose so far?"

"Half."

"God. And how many will you lose?"

"You should ask better how many will I save. A third. Maybe. If I'm lucky."

"And how do you stand with Tso's fish?"

"In another three weeks there'll be nothing left of the disease. So then I can take a shipment from him, but—"

"But in the meantime that's three weeks without a sale."

Milt nodded.

"How much can you get by with?"

"Ten thousand."

She looked at him piercingly.

"With five I can stall enough to keep going. I'll make you a special price."

"I don't capitalize on friends' troubles." She opened the drawer to her desk and took out her checkbook.

Without warning a needlelike pain shot through her left eye.

"Okay?" Milt said.

She felt jangled. "What? Oh . . . yes. Sure. Just a headache." But she wanted to get out of there and be safely battened down in her own home. She handed him a check.

"But this is six thousand," Milt said.

"Maybe you'll want some salami in your eggs."

$\triangledown$

14

NINA COULD HEAR the humid night dripping off the trees as she made her way up West Tenth Street in the fetid air that fills Manhattan in August. But few things could dampen her enthusiasm for her traditional Friday-night book hunt at Cynthia's.

How delighted she had been when she attended the opening of Cynthia's lovely bookstore Between the Lines, last July. The shop contained not a single ceiling light. Instead, authentic green-shaded library lamps threw subtle illumination on wood surfaces and brass pots of freshly cut seasonal flowers.

As if that weren't more than enough for Nina, who disliked chain bookstores with their illiterate help and too great an emphasis on best-selling authors, Cynthia stocked every book in print by many of Nina's favorite novelists.

Nina had been ecstatic to find that Cynthia understood that gardening was a way of rinsing the eye, and that one could see the entire mystery of life and old age and death in a single flower. They also shared a love of May Sarton's work. The two had immediately become friends.

Time smeared, and she was reeled back to that first drink at Cynthia's brownstone apartment. She could again feel Cynthia looking at her with a composed consideration that seemed to operate from a different state of consciousness than her words. As she moved she had been so elegant in her motion Nina thought if she were a bird she'd be a heron. Suddenly Cynthia had laughed outright. A deep, full laugh that Nina always enjoyed. There had been something different about her, something hinted at in the way she controlled her laugh—cutting it off, it seemed, a microsecond too early. Cynthia was not a person to be understood, only experienced.

Now, seeing the bookshop less than a block away, Nina was singularly proud of how she'd reacted to what happened after dinner that night. She had felt carefree, drinking chilled Vouvray, which tasted perfect with the fruit and the Brie and the hidden music of Cynthia's exquisite taste in color and books and objets d'art. More calmly than she ever imagined she could, she had taken Cynthia's lovely hand from her thigh and said, "Please don't."

"You can't deny that there's an attraction on your side."

"Not a physical one. I'm sorry. If there was, I might salvage my life. And if my inability to love any woman physically interferes with our friendship, I can't think of a sadder, more pathetic end to our relationship."

To distance herself from the shock and fear of that moment—before Cynthia had said that she hoped to continue to be friends—Nina had done something she often did to escape pain: She thought of the morning when she was a little girl going on her first train trip to Hudson, New York, with her mother to visit her aunt Marie. Poppa had driven them to the train station. With a bottle of Windex he had washed the train window so she could see the river.

When she'd cried and said she didn't want to leave him and his fish room, he'd produced a goldfish in a miniature plastic bowl saying, "Now you're bringing a part of the fish room with you."

May you rest in peace, Poppa, she said to herself now, and may there be lots of fishes in heaven that you've never seen on earth.

She walked up the steps of the bookshop. When she opened the door, a bell chimed and the man reading a book behind the counter looked up. The yellow light from the lamp falling on his features made him appear malarial. To

add to the effect, his face seemed to be twisted into something she knew a great deal about: crippling shyness.

When she closed the door behind her and turned, she
realized that he had Cynthia's delicate features and her lithe
body. He was, no doubt, Paul, the painter brother whom
Cynthia adored. She'd said he would be visiting by summer's
end. Had another season already passed?

He looked helplessly at her with eyes like sunlight on
hyacinths, and a scalding fear spread from her throat and
over her breasts.

"C-can I—" he began. "I mean, is there anything—?"

As he spoke his short brow became contorted with thick
frowns, and he blushed. He lowered his head, and she
thought of an emaciated bull struggling to push a boulder.
Despite all his discomfort, she had the distinct sense that
he wanted to be near her.

When he came toward her—not hurrying—her heart was
beating so hard she was sure he would hear it.

His smile was not his sister's: It was young and without
guile.

"Cynthia t-told me about you."

She fought feeling dispersed, scattered. She tried to lift her
heart by concentrating on a blue-green band of sunlight
marbling an oak pedestal and spotlighting two sprays of
white lilies with maroon pollen on their stamens. No! She
would not have her past failures with men crash in on her
again and knot her tongue. She was a businesswoman,
well-read—

The chiming of the front door made her grab the teak
counter for support. She could feel her hair soaking through.

The customer, a middle-aged woman, meandered down
one of the planked-wood aisles.

When Paul played Mozart on the stereo then, she was
convinced it was to give them back their sense of aloneness.
Mozart was her favorite.

The shop grew dark. Was the day over or was it just a
cloud?

Reaching far down in herself she managed to blurt, "Some kind of blizzard, isn't it?" She extended her arm toward the leaded glass window, where the faces of passersby reflected the tormenting heat.

At first his bull-self was stunned. Then his eyes lit with a startling light that tripped her heart again.

"Y-yes," he uttered. "I heard there's already been a half dozen cases of snowblindness."

A sudden schoolgirl hilarity took her. And with it a smile crossed Paul's lips that grew into a grin and eventually laughter. It was the same rich, full-of-life laugh Cynthia had.

Then the late afternoon light flowed back into the shop like a pardon. And time opened out before her as it had never done before.

15

" ' $\top$ HE WIDOWMAKER,' " Carmina said, "I like that."
She set the newspaper down and looked again into the mirror
at her new frosted light brown hair color. Police reports had
mentioned a brunette, redhead, and blond.

The newspaper had used words like "sexy" and
"glamorous" to describe her, so she would have to pass up
her more provocative outfits. Instead she would dress like
Miss Goody Two Shoes with the least possible makeup. She
would not appear available—until, of course, she sighted her
prey. Her clothing, her walk, her speech, would all have to
be at odds with the published reports of the Widowmaker.

She'd transform herself into an ingenue. Many men were
excited by innocence. Look at all the X-rated films about
cheerleaders and girls in tartan school skirts. She would behave
as virginally as a woman of her age could get away with.

There was a shop near Bloomingdale's on Lexington and
Fifty-sixth Street that sold the kind of clothes she'd need:
full white crinkled cotton dresses that reached the ankle,
demure embroidered necklines, shoes with modest heels,
maybe even penny loafers if she could keep a straight face.

When she returned she carried in a shopping bag a
cream-colored batiste dress with balloon sleeves—perfect!

The police could be surveilling hotels in Manhattan. She
picked up the phone book and looked under "Motels." An
ad for the Camelot Inn near LaGuardia caught her eye. There
was an outdoor pool and a bar and disco. Most important
was the phrase, "The convenient convention spot."

She punched in the number of the inn.

"Camelot, how may I help you?"

"This is Dorine Cronin, president of Cronin Cosmetics. I understand you cater to conventions."

"Yes, ma'am. Would you like to speak to the person in charge?"

"That won't be necessary. Could you give me an idea of the kind of conventions you host?"

"Well—looking at our list for this month we have the limo drivers' meeting next week—"

"Anything sooner?"

"Right now we have Union five eighty-four."

"What's that?"

"Milk dealers. But they're in the process of checking out. We have another group checking in today."

"Who're they?"

"Amoco dealers."

"Perfect."

"Beg your pardon?"

"I meant the motel seems perfect. I'll get back to you."

Carmina sat at the Camelot Inn bar. Outside jets *rhummed* and expired like fired shells. The air-conditioning was ideal and made the air wonderfully fresh, like a cold white wine.

Next to her stood a short, thin young man with green eyes too close together and fair hair cropped short and brushed off his skeletal face. His mustache was sparse and tentative like the rest of him. He dressed and groomed as she imagined a middle-management trainee would. He wore no wedding ring, nor was there a faint circle on his fourth finger indicating he had recently removed a ring. But until a married one came along she'd play with him.

When she caught his eyes on hers she looked away demurely. Then let his eyes see her watching him.

A look of awareness sprang up in his eyes. He sat down next to her.

"Bob Dinnerman. Can I buy you a drink?"

His lips were the color of boiled lamb. She looked down at his shoes.

"Are you a cop?" she said.

"No. Do I look like one?"

"There are a lot of cops who don't look the part." Especially, she thought, since they dropped the height requirement and permitted facial hair. But he didn't look like any kind of cop, old or new school.

She could feel his heat. She sat purposefully letting the silence hang in the air like smoke. He didn't realize it but he no longer belonged to his mother or his girlfriend or anyone else. He belonged to her if she chose to take him.

His face was pink and smooth without any lines of character or experience.

"I'll have a margarita," she finally offered.

He downed his whiskey neat, as if it were chilled water on a hot day.

"Would you like something to eat?" he said. "I'm starving."

She could tell he had been drinking heavily. It showed in the glassiness of his eyes.

"Why not?"

She allowed him to think he was leading her to a red Naugahyde banquette.

After he was seated she stood, came around the table, and sat beside him.

"Now we're both on the same side," she said.

The surrender in his crooked smile made blood thicken in her veins.

He was from Dayton, where he owned the first of many—he hoped—Amoco stations.

"Having fun?" she said.

"Actually I just got into town."

"So you're checked into this motel?"

"Couldn't get any closer to the convention. Nice little room right down the hall."

"How old are you, Bob?"

"Twenty-four. Almost. I never did get your name."

"Penny."

He was fervent and optimistic about everything: the new business his father had helped him buy along with the money he'd been saving since he was sixteen pumping gas and then as a mechanic. He was going to own a chain of Amocos clear across America. Find him a wife who liked to travel like him. Raise a family.

At times his enthusiasm made him attempt to talk over the sound of a jet passing overhead. Other times he stammered getting his plans out. He laughed at himself.

She could tell that he hadn't been corrupted—not yet. He was still untainted, trusting.

But it wouldn't be long before he would learn to lie and cheat. His awkwardness would someday transform into swagger. His boyhood would be gone, taken over by a man whose ideals would fall before his ugly turkey-neck-and-gizzard dick.

She pressed her thigh up against his. The feeling repelled her. Only his pants, his shorts, and her dress separated their flesh. Soon there would be no separation.

He spilled his drink. After the waiter mopped it up and brought another she said, "I like you. I like how honest you are. Don't be nervous."

His eyes swam for a moment, and then he jumped to his feet.

"I-I like you too, but I'd better be going. I mean you can certainly charge anything you'd like to eat to my room." He pulled out his room key, dropped it, picked it up. "It's one-oh-eight."

She gave him her best smile. Then she took his hand and drew him down close to her.

"It's your girlfriend you're guilty about, isn't it Bob?"

"Yes."

"She's nice, huh?"

"She's the nicest person I've ever known."

He was back in the booth now.

"What's her name?"

"Ginny."

She waited for a jet to pass. "Is Virginia a virgin, Bob?"

"Well—not exactly. But I feel kind of funny talking about her."

She raised her palm.

She knew now that he was hers. The risk of what she was soon to do made her sap rise warm and thick.

She pressed her mouth close to his ear and whispered, "I'm sopping wet, Bob."

The expression in his face when she leaned back made breathing suddenly more difficult, as if her lungs had lost a bit of their capacity to expand.

"I—can't," he managed. "I respect her and—"

She whispered in his ear.

"You're not serious!" he said.

The widening of his pupils made her heart beat as though she were running uphill.

"I was never more serious. Never." The back of her blouse was plastered to the space between her shoulder blades. "Here."

She took his hand and placed it under her dress.

"I'm tight as a knife wound," she whispered.

When he began moving his fingers inside her a definite tingling began to take place between her legs. The arousal came not from his clumsy hand but from what she knew awaited him in the vial in her purse.

"You must try my Manhattans—they're to die for."

"L-let's go to my room, and I'll order up some whiskey and vermouth."

She smiled at his vanished fidelity. They never held onto it for long—just until their pricks took over.

With her pulse pounding in her throat and temples, she put one arm around his puny back and let him lead her away.

16

KATE HAD DRIVEN into the city with Josh for today's briefing, since he had a meeting with his astronomy society at the Hayden Planetarium. It was a blessedly temperate August day, the fine weather having drawn armies of people out of office buildings and into the greenery of Central Park. Kate and Josh bought plates of frittata from a take-out place and joined the exodus.

They sat eating and watching while mimes, jugglers, and musicians entertained. The air smelled of souvlaki and pigeons. A young man rode by on a mountain bike, outfitted as if for the Tour de France.

As a black man dressed as a clown began fashioning animal shapes out of long, skinny balloons Josh said, "The nice parts of Manhattan."

"Yeah," she said, beckoning him with her eyes to notice the man who stood not ten yards behind them urinating on an elm.

"Jesus," Josh said, seeing the man and putting his food down on the bench with disgust. "How did we ever stand that when we lived here?"

"You get anesthetized."

"Right. So. We've lived in the city and the country. Where do we go now?"

"You go to your meeting, and I hail a cab to One Police Plaza. Then we rendezvous at Bermudian and decide."

Bermudian was a restaurant in the Village where they'd eaten once a week for years.

"Yes," he said. "We can eat conch chowder and remember Bermuda—hey, are you getting randy on me the first day out of the country?"

"Does Barbie have a plastic tush?"

The sun had turned a sullen orange, and a heat inversion had set in.

She hailed a battered yellow taxi that advertised air-conditioning on its dome.

The inside of the cab was an inferno.

"Would you please turn on the air conditioner?" Kate said.

The driver had a hatchet face. He smelled of sweat and what—falafel?

"We will stall in traffic with heat," he said in an unfamiliar accent that sounded Middle Eastern.

"So why don't you shut off the air-conditioning sign?"

"It is broken. Just as this city." He cackled.

When he learned where she was going he sped off, throwing her back against her seat.

"This Widowmaker—you heard of him?"

"I've heard of that person," she said resignedly.

"In my country we do not have such people. We cut off the arms of thieves. Men as him we cut off what is cause of problem."

"Lovely."

"You like that, yes?"

In the front window she could see that he looked positively merry. Even if she had to walk downtown in the heat she needed to say, "I like that, no. Please, I need some quiet if you don't mind. And why aren't you taking the FDR? It's shorter than going through the streets."

"An accident makes traffic for FDR."

When they passed through the Village she grew nostalgic, seeing the quieter streets with no skyscrapers and the brownstone houses with gardens and curls of wrought iron. But the razor-wire roofs and iron-barred windows made her recall her earlier conversation with Josh. She feared he'd say yes to where she wanted to move only for her sake.

Approaching the Brooklyn Bridge, she was again surprised to see the unexpectedly contemporary and tastefully designed red brick building that is One Police Plaza. "With a landscaped sculpture garden, no less," as Josh would say.

Casey had moved today's meeting from the briefing room to a larger space called a team area to accommodate the additional detectives he'd assigned to the task force. Kate was delighted to see some familiar faces like serial-killer specialist Wally Mackin and his partner Frank Perkowski, who had helped her find Carl Nasson, the "Lauren Bacall Killer," who had kidnapped her niece Jenny and nearly killed the teenager.

"Somebody please tell me we got something new," Casey began.

A few moments of silence passed. Kate looked over the detectives in short-sleeved shirts and blouses, weapons clipped to their belts as they squirmed in their institutional green plastic chairs. She thought of how ingeniously Casey had laid the onus on the detectives. If nothing else, that would get their attention.

"What about the digitalis?" Casey said. "Have we hit all the medical supply companies?"

"Not all yet, Chief," said Mackin, who had eyes like curdled milk squinting out of his fierce expression. "There's a ton of 'em."

"Well, keep pushing. We got little else. What about decoys, Steers?"

A burly man stood. He wore a permanently doubtful look. "The area's just too big. Manhattan was bad enough. Now we got Queens and God knows where else. Also, the perp's not into specifics like street people or nurses or hookers. There's no connection between the victims except they were all married with kids. Now we don't even have that. Too much city, Chief."

"All right, keep on it. All we need is one break. Perkowski?"

The detective's jowled and wattled face shook as he jumped to his feet.

"Yes, sir."

"I want the entire city, including Queens, Brooklyn, the Bronx, Staten Island, even Long Island, papered with mock-ups of what he'd look like if he made his hair gray or shaved his damned head." He began pacing. "Nobody ever called this beauty a grounder—"

Kate smiled. Her detective father had taught her the baseball-slang cops' word for an easily solved murder case when she was a teenager.

"—but," Casey continued, "with the experience and brains and guts in this room it won't be long. Especially since the killer broke the MO with a single guy. Dr. Berman here is going to answer any questions you might have. And don't be afraid to look stupid. *That's* stupid with a serial hoople on our hands. Kate?"

Kate was still smiling about "hoople"—a word her father had also used to describe a crazy person.

"First," she began, "let's take your questions about this change from married victims with children to a single man. Comments, anybody? Yes, Kelsey."

"My question isn't about that. This is probably dumb, but why did the killer go to the trouble of changing hair color and length to look like Sister Mary and go to Queens to do a single guy this time—to throw us off—but still fold the twenty the same way in the lapel and use digitalis so we know it's him?"

Notebooks appeared.

"Okay," Kate said. "The killer changed hair color and length and went to Queens so as not to be caught *before* the crime. The folded bill and the digitalis are part of a drama we don't know about yet, which the killer needs. Otherwise, murdering anyone in any kind of way would do.

"But I don't believe the killer chose a single man to throw us off. I think the need to kill in this ritualized way has grown more intense. The killer's logic, I believe, says a single man will soon be a married man with kids. The victim may have even said as much."

"So," Kelsey said, "our killer's next victim might even be a boy?"

"Theoretically, yes. But I think we've got a while before, God forbid, we ever see that. Frank?"

Detective Perkowski said, "I think I understand what you said. But we know serials are able to learn from experience and change their behavior. So why does this one stay with the digitalis and folded bills to link the killings together?"

More notebooks.

"Because it feels too good to change. At this point, anyway."

Perkowski went on, "What about the risk factor? We know that multiples usually take greater and greater risks as the killings continue, because the risk intensifies their pleasure. Is that part of why this one keeps the same MO?"

"I don't think so. This killer needs this MO. It's a kind of ritual, maybe a ceremony repeating the past. A past injustice to the killer that's exorcised with the killing. Any more questions? Yes, Wally."

Detective Mackin's fierce expression had turned quizzical.

"I never understood why devoids who can't feel like normal people kill. Why, Kate, if there's no pleasure?"

"Devoids aren't entirely without emotion. The tiny spark they *can* feel can really explode when they experience extremes of behaviors like killing. With killing even the killer's body changes involuntarily. You were in combat in 'Nam, Wally. Mind telling us about some of those changes?"

"Well," he said quietly, "your mind, your body, kind of separate and then fuse—and everything becomes very clear even in all the confusion—you feel like . . . like your empty stomach is filling—God, is that what the serials want—crave?"

"Exactly. Imagine not being able to feel anything—joy, excitement, serenity. Every day is the same dullness, and then you find something—killing—that makes you feel intensely, in fact exquisitely satisfied. You're hooked."

"Why the sex before killing?" Kelsey said.

"To devoids victims are things, not people. And since sex, like murder, is a way to control—even the thought of such control excites some devoids. Imagine never getting aroused unless there's an imminent murder."

"The doctor doesn't mean imagine now, Kelsey," Casey yelled.

The room exploded into laughter. Kate was delighted. Laughter helped people to keep concentrating so they could absorb more information.

There was a knock on the door. Casey opened it, then turned back inside and called, "How about a coffee and Danish break, Kate?"

"Anything but prune."

"Good. This'll give Kelsey some more imagining time."

A half hour later Kelsey began the questioning:

"Is it true that these devoids, rakes, serials, all were sexually abused as kids?"

"It's safe to say that all were abused. Yes. Not necessarily sexually, though. Not even physical abuse. There's another kind of abuse just as horrifying, just as crippling. It leaves no scars but on the heart and mind.

"One of the worst serials I ever worked with was never struck as a child but his mother would lock him in the closet. When she let him out the child had lost his voice and was bleeding from blood vessels that had burst in his throat as a result of screaming for hours."

The room was hushed as Kate went on.

"Verbal manipulation and dishonesty can also be painful as clubs. In fact many of my colleagues agree that this is the most excruciating of abuses."

There was not a sound, not even the scratchings of pens and pencils.

$\triangledown$

17

"TODAY'S THE DAY," Josh said, handing Kate her morning cup of coffee.

It charmed Kate that he always used the same expression when they were going to see her niece Jenny. Since Kate's brother-in-law's fatal heart attack nineteen years ago, following her sister's death the year before, she and Josh had raised the girl. Kate could not imagine either of them loving her more.

They sat drinking their coffee for a while, enjoying the quiet and the anticipation. Each knew that silence was as crucial to communication as speech.

Josh said, "I didn't tell you, but when Jen phoned yesterday she said she had another one of those panic attacks she used to get right after we caught him. Poor sweetheart."

"Him" was the Lauren Bacall killer, who had kept Jenny captive for weeks before Kate and Josh and Casey had found and rescued her.

Kate's throat pained from constriction. "I suspect she'll always suffer from her memories about. . . that."

It was too painful to even say "him," let alone "Carl Nasson."

Josh excused himself to go to the bathroom, and her mind leaped back three years to those tormenting months after Jenny's rescue. The girl's panic attacks, asthmatic episodes, frequent urination, bouts of depression, fatigue, and confusion had not responded to medical or psychological treatment. After blood was discovered in her urine, they had taken her to the Mayo Clinic.

One morning Josh said, "Mayo Clinic or not, I don't buy what they're saying. Blood in the urine is not psychosomatic. I think in her case it's somatopsychic."

"Her body influencing her brain?"

"I think we've overlooked the simple. Allergies. Environmental illness."

"But she's always been able to digest bricks."

"Yes, but she's been allergic to penicillin and sensitive to MSG and caffeine, just like your sister."

After much research they found an allergist in Buffalo who used extracts for testing to which only a safe saline solution had been added.

For seven months they took turns driving the eight hours to Buffalo for accelerated testing on Fridays, Saturdays, and part of Sundays.

After a time the doctor built up her immune system. Vitamins, mineral supplements, digestive enzymes, and antigens increased her immunity to foods and chemicals to which she had grown allergic.

Jenny grew to think of Buffalo as the place in which she got well. So it didn't surprise Kate or Josh when she decided to go to college there.

When Josh returned from the bathroom, Kate said, "Sometimes I wonder if it was such a good idea for her to study criminology."

He bit into a scone, chewed, swallowed. "It was her idea. What could we do—forbid her? Besides, you said yourself it could be therapeutic. I think you were right."

She sipped her coffee. Then moved around the leftover bagel on her plate idly. "I get scared sometimes. She's trying too hard to be like us—criminology, astronomy—"

He reached over and took her hand. "She loves us. More important, she likes us. What's wrong with a child sharing interests with people she likes?"

"I don't want to be a fallen idol."

"Then cut down on your booze and drugs."

"I'm serious."

"Too damn serious if you ask me, on a 'Today's the day' day."

Her mouth formed a smile. He was delighted to see her eyes follow suit.

They sat silently for a while. Josh sensed something and looked over at Kate, who was smiling.

"What?" he said.

"Just thinking of what she said when I took her home crying from her first day in kindergarten."

Josh said, " 'But I *already* know how to play, Aunt Kate!' "

"You should be pressed in a book."

"Thank you." He stood and bowed dramatically. "Now that's how *I* take being an idol."

"Well put your idol tush into gear. Otherwise we'll miss our plane, and Jenny . . ." Her voice trailed.

"What?"

"What if she doesn't like the idea?"

"Then we'll both be fallen idols."

▽

18

As ALWAYS, JENNY was the first person in line as they stepped from the ramp to the arrival gate at Buffalo International Airport.

"Hi!" she called, walking toward them with the same bold bouncy step her mother had had.

"Hi to you!" said Kate, beaming at the sight of the combination of girl and woman with ingenuous face and wise eyes.

When Jenny came into her arms, Kate felt she was hugging her niece, daughter, and friend.

Afterward Kate watched as her two favorite people embraced. She loved the way the young woman dressed— hunter green cable-knit cotton sweater that matched her eyes and nondesigner jeans so worn by wear and washing they were as soft to the touch as the underbelly of a bird.

"Have I got a surprise for you," Josh said.

Jenny looked at Josh. "You had a Nestlé's Crunch, right?"

"Damn! A man can't get any privacy from that sense of smell of yours."

"You'd better control that sweet tooth," Kate said to Josh. "You've put on a nice few pounds."

Once they had settled in her Volkswagen Beetle—she had had a friend who was on vacation in Mexico buy and drive it home—Jenny said, "Hey, what's with the nose-against-the-glass, Aunt Kate? You act like you've never shuffled off to Buffalo before."

The older two looked into each other's faces.

Josh said, "It's just that knowing you live here makes the place so friendly, you know?"

"I hardly like you guys at all."

In the backseat, next to Josh, Kate leaned forward, resting her chin on the top of the front seat, and stared down at an air purifier that got its power from an outlet in the dashboard. Jenny was still allergic to gasoline fumes. Kate looked at Jenny's twiglike fingers on the steering wheel with their jaundiced cast, a sign of her illness.

Jenny said, "Aunt Kate?"

"S-sorry," Kate said, remembering throwing out every carpet in the house and shopping endlessly through mail-order catalogs for charcoal masks and flours with names like *spelt* and *teff*. "Where are we?"

"On the one-ninety."

"Why is it," Josh said, "you Buffalonians always put the definite article 'the' before every noun? Like 'traffic is heavy on the one-ninety.' Or 'let's go to the B-Quick for a six-pack'?"

Jenny laughed.

Kate smiled and said, "And you call your soda 'pop' and refer to the Bills as 'us.' "

"I'll tell you what, though," Jenny said. "You won't find realer people. Even the women here eat like humans instead of birds. No spinach leaves with lemon juice for brunch here. Even our salad bars have wings and roast beef and—wait a minute—"

Kate turned to Josh, smiling. She winked.

Jenny glanced at her in the rearview mirror. "You're kidding!" she screamed.

"Careful," Josh said.

Jenny went on in disbelief. "You've been hating the little gossipy minds in Rhinebeck, and you said you had a surprise for me. Is it true? Did I guess it? You're thinking of moving to Buffalo?"

"Only if we wouldn't be crowding you, sweetheart," Kate said.

"Crowding? Why, this is the best thing that's happened since I was told I could eat fruit again."

Josh saw the water in Kate's eyes and put his arm round her taut shoulder. "Kind of like an empty nest—in reverse."

All three began to laugh.

Then they continued speaking, interrupting, making plans, so absorbed in their bliss they missed their exit.

Finally, when they stepped out of the Beetle, Jenny said, "I know something you don't know about the Widow-maker."

19

"I . . . DON'T KNOW," the madam said, rising from behind a desk Carmina thought would be considered ornate even at Versailles.

She watched the older woman with pancake makeup over reptilian skin dig a pack of cigarettes from a pocket in her harem outfit and light one. The outfit was one hundred percent gold lamé, she'd say that for the bitch. And earlier she'd noticed that one of the hookers in the red velvet "fantasy room" outside was wearing what was certainly a real silk toga.

"What do you mean, you don't know? Is there something wrong with my looks? I mean the beauties outside aren't exactly ready to parade down the platform in Atlantic City."

The madam picked a piece of tobacco off her tongue, rolled it between her fingers, and dropped it onto the fuchsia pile rug. "Those girls are the best earners I've ever had. You're pretty enough. It's just . . . your hair, what color would you say it is?"

"Magenta."

"Yeah. Magenta hair, black nails . . . I don't know."

The swastika earrings Carmina had discovered in the East Village swung as her head followed the buxom woman, who paced now, lighting another cigarette from the butt of the previous one.

Without warning a picture beamed into her mind. She saw herself as Nina at six, being led through the night by her father to the secret house where Poppa danced with the ladies who gave her candy.

For a moment Carmina was certain she could smell that

undeniable combination of odors of perfume and candy and whiskey and cigarette smoke. Then, suddenly, she could also smell the rancid stench that had come from Poppa's garage. And for a moment she saw, flashing behind her eyes, Them with Their horny plates and then torn pieces of color, and instantly her entire body trembled and her insides writhed as if all her nerve endings had suddenly been severed and alcohol poured on them.

"Can you dress up in any other looks? I mean the place isn't called Fantasies for nothing. My girls have to be, use, variety, you know?"

Carmina looked out of Nina's girlish eyes. Slowly she recognized the madam and who she herself was.

"Yes, I know. I can be anyone they want. A Donna Reed librarian type with glasses and a Peter Pan collar with a black leather whip in my book bag. A wild Viking wench with fur boots up to my crotch who can lick a man till he thinks his balls have turned into satin."

"Great! Go ahead, tell me more."

"I can be everywoman and any woman. I can be as submissive as an ancient Chinese with bound feet. Or as detached as an Aryan ice maiden who makes them want to nail her to the cross."

The madam's mouth was agape, her red tongue lolling as though she were poised to catch a fly.

"—I can be innocent, sophisticated, debauched and wanton. I can be their whore or their sister or their mother or even their brother—stick my finger up their ass as they're riding home and—"

"Terrific! Where the hell did you learn to talk so sexy—a sex phone service?"

"Johns are my life's work."

The woman threw her cotton-candy strawberry blond hair back, pulled a chair over, and made a motion that seemed to Carmina like brushing away her tail before she sat. "Yeah, you just might work out. Besides, what do I have to lose?"

Only a customer, Carmina thought, letting the great lizard of a woman see her smile.

*   *   *

Later that night, when the madam had grown curious after Carmina had been with one of the regulars for close to an hour and a half, she knocked on the door of the bedroom she had assigned her.

When no one answered, she knocked a second time. And then a third. There was no response so she opened the door. She lost her dinner when she saw the contorted john on the floor and the open window by which the new bitch had obviously left.

She locked the door behind her, washed, and drank four fingers of vodka over ice. She shook as if she had stood too long before a freezer, then took two more inches of Stoli, straight this time.

She returned to the room where the dead john was. Repulsed, she made herself close his eyes so she wouldn't have to see the hell that was still plain in them. He still had a hard-on, which didn't surprise her.

She went through all his pockets, keeping the $258 in his wallet as a reward for her discomfort.

When she noticed a folded-up double sawbuck in his lapel pocket, she shivered. That new bitch was probably the killer everybody was talking about in the papers and on TV. A woman!

She punched in the number of the asswipe in the Genovese family she was supposed to phone when a john died on the premises.

The wipe told her to close for business early, and he would pick up the stiff rolled in a carpet. She told him she thought the killer was the Widowmaker. In a voice so hard it made her aware of the fillings in her teeth, he ordered, "Like I told you before. We don't want no annecessary puh-blicity. You dint see nothing, you don't say nothin' to nobody, or you're furt-erlizer."

What a mess, she thought, and put the twenty with the rest.

∇

20

"THE 'HOW' IS your job, Uncle Josh," Jenny said as she rubbed chicken breasts with garlic and ginger root. "The 'Why' is yours, Aunt Kate."

"And yours?" Kate said.

On the CD player Jenny's favorite James Taylor segued into Barbara Cook—Josh and Kate's favorite:

"Ain't love easy/When it's you babe . . ."

"My usual job," Jenny said, "is to act as a kind of instant devil's advocate, forcing you two to dig down deeper to prove your points. To speed up your hunches into scientific theories."

With the skilled grace she loved about him, Josh succeeded during the microsecond Jenny averted her gaze to the lettuce soup to show Kate the pride he felt in the young woman.

"I want to talk about my profile of the killer," Jenny said. "Why don't we go into the living room."

Jenny's two-bedroom house had belonged to a woman in her environmental illness support group. She was so sick she had moved to the Arizona desert, where she now lived in a glass and tile and metal house on a ceramic foundation.

As they entered the living room Josh said, "Every time I come into this room I feel like I'm going back into another century. Oak furniture, cotton drapes, Oriental rug, wrought-iron magazine rack, ceramic lamps with silk shades, glass-doored bookcases. Nothing plastic, everything natural. I think if more of contemporary life were lived like this I wouldn't spend so much time imagining distant galaxies."

Kate smiled lovingly at Josh. "Now tell us your theory about the killer, Jen."

"Just one thing more." She left and returned in moments with a bottle of champagne and three fluted glasses, saying, "It's not every day my two favorite Earthlings decide to move in."

"Now wait," Kate said, "we didn't even consider moving *in* on you. We'll find a house nearby and—"

"This is my house. You gave it to me. I'd be hurt if you lived anywhere else."

Josh said, "We're not moving anywhere till after this case is solved. So let's get to that champagne."

Josh popped the cork and Jenny poured, giving herself a thimbleful. She raised her glass. "As Dom Perignon said at the moment of his discovery of the bubbly—"

" 'Come quickly. I am tasting stars!' " Josh and Kate joined in.

"I think I know why our friend Casey hasn't been able to trace the digitalis from medical supply sources."

"How'd you know about that?" Kate said.

"He told me."

"So," Josh said, "where's the digitalis coming from?"

"Foxglove."

"Clever," said Josh.

"Very," said Kate. "You may be right."

"In these cases," Josh said, "I'm the 'How' and Kate is the 'Why.' Now you're becoming the 'What.' "

"Right. What do you *really* think about the case, Aunt Kate?"

"I think we need another member in our family to tell us the 'Who'!"

21

Some fishes produce an egg, which develops without
fertilization by a male—parthenogenesis. In fact, such
a species has no mate at all.

NINA SLAMMED SHUT the coffee-table book called *Fishes*.
Why, when her first two dates with Paul had been nothing
less than perfect, was she sitting here feeling sorry for
herself? Maybe, another part of her said, because one day, if
it keeps getting louder, I'm afraid he'll hear my biological
clock ticking away.

No! No way was she going to worry about that now.
Expect a miracle.

Then she remembered Paul was cooking dinner for them
in Cynthia's apartment while she was spending the weekend
with a friend.

Thinking about what to wear, she felt a cold, briny
dampness suddenly descend on her. What if one day she saw
in Paul's eyes the disappointment and ridicule she had seen
in Ralph Weir's?

Easy, she thought. Paul seemed to like how she'd dressed
so far. She was tired of exhausting herself considering what
to wear each time they saw each other, as if the wrong blouse
or dress would make a failure of their evening. If the glue
between them could be undone by fashion, she would learn
to live without Paul. She would wear jeans and a sweater and
be done with it.

Suddenly the brightness of the afternoon failed. Instead

of sitting in the garden to contemplate the changing light, which relaxed her, she interpreted the growing dimness as a metaphor for her fading youth and fecundity.

The sense of doom that followed made her lie on the couch from the weight of it. Then, determined to fight her mood, she bolted up, watered the houseplants, and fed the birds and the fishes.

Peace returned. Vacuuming, for example, never had this effect, but serenity had always resided for her in the natural world. Machines did things outside the natural rhythm of life. But gardening or cooking or feeding living things—anything that couldn't be rushed—always gave her back her balance.

In the days before the Widowmaker she would've walked the few blocks to Cynthia's apartment in the crisp autumn air. Now she phoned for a private taxi.

While she waited, the thought that Paul might try to make love to her tonight delighted and alarmed her. She had almost no experience, knew no technique. And even though his good-night kisses were quick, there was an undercurrent of heat in them that ignited and frightened her.

She gathered the wine bottles for dinner.

Paul had put a Mozart disc on the CD player and lit candles that blazed on strategically placed bouquets of gold tulips, which gave the apartment a festive atmosphere. There was a new flush to his gaunt cheeks that both panicked and excited her, as did his haunting new scent—somewhere between lime and something much more tropical.

During dinner (corn and crab chowder, watercress, endive and walnut salad, and garlic shrimp over angel hair pasta) she said, "I miss the spring and summer. You?" God, she thought, I'm actually resorting to talking about the weather!

"I-I'm re-lieved," he said, "after the unrelenting summer."

"This dinner," she said, grateful for this man who could even raise the subject of weather above small talk. "I wish I could cook so elegantly."

"Cynthia says she's never had better food outside of Italy. Would you make your mussels marinara for me sometime, please?"

Where had she met such a man? she thought, noting he had lost his stutter entirely now. She was bereft, for it had protected her from his more sophisticated self. She felt naked and inept.

"I love the fall," he said, "the stirring of sap in the maples—"

And in you?

She didn't know if she had thought or said the last.

"Please tell me," she said, "about your paintings. How I wish that I could see them." This was true. His paintings, she had a sense, would prove a window through which she could gaze on the most meaningful depths of him.

"So do I. I . . . mean that you could . . ."

"I know what you mean," she said feeling again that superb clicking in of relaxation that always came when she was with Paul long enough. Dear man. "What's it like for you—painting? Who, what, do you like? Listen to me! God I hate what my mouth does to me sometimes."

"Well, don't look at me as if I have a speech impediment, p-p-p-please."

Nina began a laugh that emerged as a groan. Paul deliberately groaned, and they burst out laughing. The laughter grew deeper and more boisterous, lifting and casting out any hesitancy in the air.

Paul led her to the couch where he served espresso and iced chocolate cake.

"So?" she said.

"So what?"

"So what about painting? Talk to me." Talk to me forever.

"I started out wanting to be a novelist. I got tired of always having to keep my head on the damn story. I wanted to just indulge in language, words. Now I can indulge myself in form and color and light.

"I love experiencing myself without words. No, without

story, I should say. Mostly I love the quality of light in some paintings. The way it dances about in some Dutch rooms by Vermeer. A lemony light by Culp on two wineglasses. Sorry, I didn't mean to go on."

"I'm sorry you stopped. I never realized till now that light draws me into paintings, too. One thing?"

"Yes. Please. Anything."

She was afraid of all the need she saw in his face. Yet her own need kept her from withdrawing from the personality of the conversation. "I think," she said, "I would hate to give up a painting I had gotten just as I wanted it. A writer keeps his work."

"You don't have to have your work on a wall or an easel to keep it."

"Of course. You're right. I didn't mean to imply—"

"Don't do that. Please."

Had she once again made a blind blunder with a man? *Not this man* . . . It was a prayer. "What?" she was finally able to dredge up.

"You're a lovely sensitive woman, one of the smartest people I've ever met. Don't do what I did for years. Mistake sophistication for grace of living. Grace is in living in the world with beauty. With flowers and birds. The people I know with the most grace are those who've had hard times. When they're happy there's no smugness about being the right kind of happy in it. It's not inclusive or exclusive. Cynthia's one of those people. So are you. I hope I can become one of you."

She felt his lips on her own then, not hesitant yet not demanding. And her whole being reached out to him as if to a warm, clear light that simultaneously drew out and reflected the best in her. Then a clicking sound.

When she opened her eyes she saw that the clicking was the rain beating on the window. Maple leaves sifted down one by one, floating with the notes of Mozart's music. She sensed how simply the trees let go, let fall their riches, and were rewarded with renewal.

"For once when I need it," he said, "my tongue isn't glued to my mouth. There's too much trying for sophistication and too little quality. You're quality, Nina. You're what I need."

Her heart darted in her breast then.

Without any hesitation she looked deeply into his eyes and slowly, without hesitation, removed her earrings.

"Hurry, darling," she said. *Before the world has a chance to crash in on us.*

▽

22

Nora's nipples were as brown as her eyes. Such perfectly oval eyes the color and sheen of a broth made from mahogany. Casey had never seen prettier eyes. She lifted the hair off his forehead now and kissed the skin underneath. Licked it. So full of new ways he'd never imagined! She licked down his face, his chest, until his penis beat against her face and then she—

"Chief?"

Casey came out of the daydream immediately. God in heaven, that was one woman. For months after Moira had died he would wake suddenly like this after a heavy night of drinking. During that time he didn't really ever fall asleep and wake up. Instead he'd passed out and come to.

The chief grasped Commissioner Ellis's hand. It was smooth as a crow's feathers and nearly as dark. The commissioner's features, blunt and small, were set a bit too closely in his face, giving him a vulnerable look that Casey guessed had helped the ex-judge to throw many an adversary off balance in his long political career.

Barely moving his lips Ellis said, "What's that you have there—a Bloody Mary?"

Ellis had never made a negative remark about Casey's drinking. After he and Kate and Josh had taken down the Lauren Bacall Killer the commish had even sent him a case of Irish with a card that read: "I've always admired Lincoln for answering the critics of Grant's drinking by sending the general a case of bourbon. I hope the enclosed keeps you anything but dry."

"It's a Virgin Mary," Casey said.

"Acch." The commissioner winced. "No wonder this Widowmaker bastard is still skating."

"You got a point there." He left his scarlet drink. "The Irish call it 'a Bloody Shame.' "

The commissioner guffawed, showing his prominent front teeth. They were large and slightly bucked. A white person's teeth. Casey took them as proof some Caucasian had stumbled into the Ellis family woodpile.

The bartender arrived in a silk bow tie, ruffled white shirt, and black Eisenhower tuxedo jacket. What is this, Casey thought, a freaking wedding?

Ellis ordered a gimlet straight up. The "room," as the commissioner referred to it, had a black-and-white tiled floor, matte black mica bar counter, chrome-and-black-leather chairs and banquettes. There was a smoked mirror the length of the bar.

"So what do you think of the place?" Ellis said.

"Not exactly your typical bucket of blood. I feel like I'm up to my tits in Yuppies."

When the commissioner only smiled at what Casey had expected to be good for at least one Ellis-guffaw, the chief said, "One of those another-day-another-seven-homicides-in-the-Naked-City days, huh?"

"You got it. Fucking Brooklyn jury. They acquitted Ianozzi."

"You're not serious."

"I wish."

"Fuck me. Biggest dope dealer we ever got. Fucking jury would've cut Attila loose, sent him home in a medallion taxi. God in heaven. Ianozzi. Here's your whatever-you-call-it. Drink up, you'll feel better."

"Maybe you should take your own advice," said the commissioner.

Maybe he should. He still hadn't had the quota Kate and Josh had sentenced him to. He studied the bottles behind the bar, scheming to get as much jolt as possible for his two measly drinks. Shame Irish was only eighty-six proof. The bonded bourbons were still a hundred, although Wild Turkey was a hundred and one. And there was always Bacardi—one fifty-one. Was he that desperate?

"Wild Turkey," he said, "straight, water back."

"Wild Turkey, is it now?" Ellis said in his ludicrous imitation of a Gaelic brogue. But Casey was rapt in the beauty of the act of the maudlin bartender pouring half his daily ration.

"My God, that's a fine color," Casey said absently.

"Not bad," Ellis said without emotion.

Casey figured Ellis's mind had slipped to the true reason for tonight's meeting: pressure to speed up the solving of the Widowmaker case. He admired the commissioner's patience in getting to the matter. In this area his superior had skill and art. Ellis's ability to use blarney was no less than a gift.

Ellis said, "The people downtown want me to run for mayor. What do you think?"

"I think you'll be a great mayor," he said, meaning it.

"Thanks. Sometimes we don't think to say what we've been feeling until it's too late. In the war of New York's Finest against the rogues—both ones who take whatever freebies happen their way and the ones who become cops only to steal—you are one hell of a good man, Case."

Casey was complimented. Ellis had never called him by his nickname before. Casey knew the rest had been said to motivate a quicker collar in the Widowmaker case, which would help Ellis politically. He had no problem with his superior's slickness. God knew he used it himself with his own people. And to reach his own station, let alone the commissioner's, required more politics than criminology.

"If I make mayor," Ellis was saying, "you can name your spot. Commissioner, if you want."

Casey set his glass down. Slick or not, Ellis always kept his word. It was good politics.

"Thanks. Really appreciate that, Ben. But I'm getting ready to put a fork in me."

"What about head of Internal Affairs?"

"Head cheese-eater? Thanks, not for me." He took another sip.

"Excuse me," Ellis said, "just thought of something."

Casey watched the commissioner take from inside his gray pinstripe suit a leather-cased notebook and a fountain pen and make a note. Casey couldn't remember the last time he'd seen a fountain pen. Shame. Beautiful things.

"Sorry," Ellis said. "You know, there's a detail not many people know about, even at your level."

"Okay," Casey said, staring forlornly at the one sip left in his glass. He shucked his coat and laid it on the stool next to him. Having refused two job offers and told Ellis about his decision to retire, he felt less formal, more friendly.

"The detail, area, whatever," Ellis said, "is supposed to look for guys who are cashing pension checks even though they're supposed to be dead, but they're not dead."

"Come again?"

"Not the men, of course. Their widows. Millions of dollars every year."

"Millions?"

"Right. But you're not interested in that kind of work, are you. Why are you getting out? Is it Nora? Lovely woman."

"Thanks. It's her. It's my family. I got grandkids I don't recognize from one visit to the next." He drained his drink and raised one finger to the bartender, who immediately responded. "You were in the war, weren't you, Ben?"

"Navy flier."

"I was a dogface," Casey said. " 'Grunts' they call them now. Anyway, after battle there was always this intense pleasure in living. The trees were alive. The grass, the dirt—everything. And you wanted to be a good man. Decent. Honest. You know what I mean."

Seeing genuine absorption on Ellis's face, he smiled. He felt he might even have found a friend. "Anyway, you're never more alive than when you've almost been killed."

"Amen, brother."

"Right. You recognize what's best in yourself and the world and how easily it can be lost." He turned to Ellis for emphasis. "And then you go on living and you lose that feeling, and you become a cop and you go up the ladder until one day the commissioner his own self offers you his job and you say no because the boys uptown have already asked you to be his honor the mayor."

Casey waited, deadpan. Finally, when he could hold back no more, he let himself laugh. "You should see your freaking face."

"Motherfucker and all his sisters. You—" and Ellis roared with laughter.

"Now," Casey said, "maybe we can get to the obligatory scene where you tell me how much pressure you're getting from the press and the mayor's office."

With this Ellis laughed so hard he spilled Casey's drink. Casey had taken only two sips. He ordered another. Two sips away from having faithfully kept his word to Kate and Josh.

When the laughing stopped Casey said, "I know what you want, Ben. And I want to give this sucker to you. I need to pick up every rock. I need more people. Shields and uniforms. More than we ever used in a net operation before. And then maybe more. I'd want freaking martial law if I could get it."

"You got whatever you need. Let's both go out with a bang."

"It's the freaking Widowmaker who's going out. Now let's eighty-six this mausoleum and go eat."

23

"K<small>ATE</small> B<small>ERMAN</small>?"

It was a strange voice, deep yet effeminate.

"Yes."

"Have you got a moment?"

"Who is this?"

"My name is Sawyer Benard."

"How did you get my unlisted number?"

"If something's important enough you find a way. Greg Haines was my best friend."

"I don't have any idea what you're talking about. And I don't have an unlisted number so I can talk to people who didn't get it from me."

"Greg Haines was murdered in a whorehouse by the Widowmaker."

"Mr. Benard, I get notes, letters, every week about murders supposedly committed by the Widowmaker."

"Greg went to the same cathouse every Friday night for the last eight years. When I went to speak to the madam she claimed she didn't know him."

"That's what good madams are supposed to do."

"Of course. But I told her all about Greg. I proved to her I wasn't a cop."

"Was your friend's body found on her premises?"

"He was found floating in the Harlem River. Typical mob killing. Everyone knows Clarice's house is owned by the mob."

"I'm sorry you lost your friend, but I'm leaving for an

appointment soon. Besides, I still don't see any connection between your friend's death and the Widowmaker case."

"Autopsy found digitalis in Greg's body."

"So?"

"So Greg ran marathons. Had a heart like a Lamborghini engine."

Pause.

"Mrs. Berman?"

"I'm here. Where can we meet?"

America was one of her favorite restaurants in Manhattan. And Kate was impressed that Sawyer Benard had suggested it.

Sitting here now waiting for him at one of a hundred tables and admiring the vast murals of the Statue of Liberty and a bald eagle soaring past a pastoral landscape, she grew nostalgic for her life in the city. And, surprising herself, she grew hungry for Vermont apple fritters or the New Orleans chicken muffulata, Philadelphia cheese steak sandwich or many of the dozens of regional specialties from all over America.

She was troubled by this meeting. Was it simply nerves? She had considered asking Josh to join her but was afraid Benard might not speak to anyone but her.

However, there was little danger in a place as public as America.

At precisely noon Kate saw a slim man of about five feet ten step through the entrance, dressed in a beige suit with a blue turtleneck under a chocolate shirt. He was holding the walking stick with a brass horsehead grip he had described on the phone.

She watched him sight her, then raised her hand.

He came toward her with the confident, springy gait of a dancer.

As he drew nearer she suspected from the monogram gracing his right shirt cuff and the exquisite tailoring of his suit that his clothes were made to measure, if not handmade.

He had wispy brown hair receding from his widow's peak
and, as if an attempt to compensate for the loss, a guards-
man's brush of a mustache.

"I'm very grateful for your coming," he said.

His voice was an icy slap. He spoke with a woman
smoker's whiskeyed huskiness, which reminded her of the
kind of voice the Lauren Bacall Killer had sought in his
victims.

She refused his offer of a Dunhill cigarette in a paper-thin
gold case.

"Mind?" he said.

She did but she wanted him relaxed, so she could learn as
much as possible about him.

He took a Chinese red lacquered Du Pont lighter from an
inside pocket in his jacket and lit a cigarette. In the butane
light his eyes were a startling green in his deeply tanned face.
It was an angular face, the features so small and thorny she
had the unsettling feeling that he was honed. And if he fell
over and she caught him, she'd be bleeding from her efforts.

"Why me?" she said. "Why didn't you go to the police?"

"Casey, you mean. One doesn't go to Inspector Lestrade
when one knows it is Holmes who's solving his cases."

"That's not even close to the truth."

"Close enough. Besides, I didn't need some homophobic
cop looking for gay psychological motives that don't exist."

He was not being bitter, just factual. And his ensuing open
smile so disarmed her that she smiled back despite herself.

"How did you get my phone number?"

"Your husband's astronomy club. I read about it in the
profile on you in *Vanity Fair*. Spoke in broken Spanish. Told
them I was phoning from Chile. Chile's the best viewing
spot in the Americas."

"I know. I'm still offended by what you did."

"I was desperate. I'm very sorry. Don't have something
alcoholic soon, my nerves are going to coalesce and I'll light
up like a Nintendo grand prize winner. Don't you just hate
the obligatory social structures we need to keep up for

strangers?" He sucked in breath. "I'm having wine. A well-rounded—no, positively fat—Pommard to mellow me out. Would you like to share some, or does your liver have a preferable poison?"

She laughed. If Benard was trying to get her to like him, he was certainly succeeding.

Later, when their waiter arrived with the wine and asked for their order, Benard said, "I've been promising myself their griddled Chesapeake crab cake on an onion roll all this terrible week, even though I know the tartar sauce will make it impossible for me to wear anything except from my fat closet."

"Well, you'll get no support from me. I'm having the Philadelphia cheese steak sandwich."

"This could be the beginning of a beautiful friendship," he said in a charming imitation of Bogart.

When their waiter left she said, "Is there any connection you see besides the digitalis between your lover and the other victims? Sorry, you wouldn't know about the others."

He swallowed a piece of Bibb lettuce and speared a disk of pickled onion.

"I know whatever I've read in the papers, which is every word I could find. Greg was a flautist with the Philharmonic. Divorced. Three kids. Originally from Society Hill, Philadelphia. I couldn't find one solitary thing that matched the others."

He absently lay down his fork. When finally he spoke, it was as though she were hearing him across a wide expanse.

"I know it must sound crazy to you, but Greg and me—we'd gotten it all together. He was bi, and we weren't naive enough to believe his need for women would just go away. I'm not telling you his Friday nights didn't hurt. But believe me, it helps when you know the woman is just a prop your man doesn't really care about."

He had picked up his fork, and his thumb was pressed white from pushing against the tines.

"We almost broke up some years ago. But AIDS came

along, and like a lot of gays we stayed together, knowing we were terrified to date other people. I guess facing our breakup made us aware of what we meant to each other— God, I loved him."

His green eyes had turned almost black. Kate was stricken by the grief she saw in his face, then wondered fleetingly if what now seemed like a hard, rigid expression was indeed grief or something else.

"Felt . . . related to him, you know?" Sawyer was saying.

"I know. What can I do to help?" she said, feeling guilty now about Casey's man, who was sitting at an adjoining table.

She watched him lift his pointy chin. His eyes were green again.

"I live off a trust fund. Never did have to learn to work. Overall I've loved having all my days to do as I please. But since Greg's murder I've wished for a career, a meaningful job to help me forget. Please let me help you find whoever killed him."

He reached across the table and took her hands in his.

"I know it sounds crazy," he went on, "but, look, I'll be a gofer. No job will be too small or too dirty. This is not just about finding Greg's killer, Kate. It's about finding my own life again. Please."

"I'll have to discuss it with my husband first." This is happening too fast, she thought, but his eyes. . . so full of pain. . .

"Bless you," he said.

▽

24

"Let me get this straight," Josh said to Kate after she had picked him up in their car at the Hayden Planetarium, "you met with a man, a total stranger, who's involved with the case?"

"In a public place. With a cop a few tables away. Right."

"Right, she says. What if this guy was a nut and hurt you—or worse—before the cop could help? Jesus, Kate."

"Hey, lighten up. And quit calling me 'she.' "

"After all you've—we've—been through with the Slasher and that *momzer* Nasson, you tell me to lighten up?" He looked at her in awe.

"Okay. You're right. Should've been more careful. Had him meet me with Casey right there or something."

"Something, yeah."

"I said you were right. Not like you to go after me like this."

After a beat he shifted closer to her, and she took his hand and squeezed.

"Scared the shit out of me," he said, hugging her right side fiercely.

"I know. Sorry, honey. C'mon now and make like the autopsy maven. I'd like to know how Jay's people determined that Greg Haines was murdered with digitalis, not by drowning."

"Jay" was Jay Springer, who had replaced Josh as Chief ME of New York City.

"When a person drowns," Josh said, "the body always ends up facing down, with the arms, legs, and face dragging against the bottom."

"Is it the same for a river as an ocean, for example? They found Haines in the Harlem River."

"In rivers with currents the face may scrape against the bottom, which forces sand and weeds into the nose."

"Yes? So?"

"So things like sand and weeds found inside the lungs show that the person did drown. But if a person was killed and then dropped into a river to make it look like an accidental drowning, there'd be no sand or weeds inside the lungs."

"Ahhh," she said. Then: "Why don't we go to Stellar Attractions?"

"What favor is it you want that you're willing to be bored again while I have multiple orgasms in my favorite astronomy shop in the world?"

While it was true she did have a favor to ask about Sawyer Benard, she also loved what Stellar Attractions italicized in Josh. Religion did not make him think of God. Stargazing did. Sometimes she could see him watching drifting motes of dust and felt he was imagining timeless galaxies.

"Foiled again," she said.

On the way to Stellar Attractions they stopped at a traffic light at Fifty-seventh Street and saw a homeless woman who had kenneled herself in a carton.

"My God, on Fifty-seventh Street," he said. "Next it'll be Park Avenue. Poor woman."

Kate looked in the gutter and saw in the stream of water running toward the sewer a tennis ball bereft of its felt, a broken Styrofoam cup, a half-eaten sandwich blackened with filth, the remains of a small bird, and a stretched-out condom. The stream and its cargo seemed a perfect microcosm of the reasons they had left this city with all its wonders.

* * *

Stellar Attractions, on West Fifty-seventh Street and Twelfth Avenue, was twenty thousand square feet—"the largest astronomy store in the world." There was one section devoted to "computer linkage" and astronomy, with computerized telescopes and software. Another section contained everything from binoculars to a $250,000 telescope. There was an area for books and magazines and another for videotapes, including classic science fiction movies like *The Martian Chronicles*, *When the Earth Stood Still*, and *When Worlds Collide*.

As she followed Josh past displays of astro cameras and telephoto lenses, she thought of how pained Sawyer Benard's face had been when he'd pleaded to be a part of the case no matter how infinitesimal.

"Look at this photo," Josh exclaimed, "of the Great Nebula in Orion. Fifteen light-years across. Twenty thousand of our solar systems could fit in there."

She looked around at the floor-to-ceiling NASA photographs of the Earth, the Moon, and the rest of the universe and felt her breath become shallow.

"And this picture of Rigel," Josh was saying, "can you imagine a star that burns with the power of fifty-seven thousand suns?"

She knew, of course, that what he was saying was truly astounding and wished she could get as emotional as he did over it.

"C'mon," he said, "let's sit down and have a coffee. I've been dragging you around long enough."

They sat in the little restaurant that was a facsimile of the USS *Enterprise*; its menu listed "Astro Specials of the Day."

"Who's this man on the cover?" she asked, pointing at her menu.

"George Alcock. A holy man. Discovered five comets and four novae and memorized twenty thousand stars."

"Jesus, he must've gotten quite a crick in his neck—"

"Very funny. We're not talking about an astrophysicist here. This guy's an amateur like me. His memorization of the Milky Way down to the eighth magnitude stands as one of the great observation feats of the twentieth cen— never mind."

"No, I'm really interested."

"What you're interested in is the other piece of this Sawyer whatever-his-name-is thing."

"I hate you. No, loathe is closer to the truth."

"Me too. So. Talk. What?"

"He was terribly in love with Greg Haines. Much more than he realized while Haines was alive. He has no career. No hobbies. God, I'm bad at this."

"He wants us to let him help with the case."

"Thank you."

"Out of the question."

"But what if we give him a few gofer jobs?"

"We don't even know this guy. It could be dangerous."

"We won't exactly be going on SWAT raids with him."

"Look, maybe I *am* overreacting because of things that happened in the past. But this makes me nervous."

"When you see how sweet he is you'll see there's nothing to worry about."

"He'll get in the way."

"We can send him on paper chases. He won't even be with us. You've got to meet him. Charming. Bright."

She saw that his resolve was melting.

"As a personal favor to me, Josh. Please."

"Well . . ."

"I'm listening."

"He'll be on probation."

"Of course."

"And this is the biggie."

"I'm still listening."

"You agree to a matinee at the Carlisle today."

"I forgot how much the celestial affects your testosterone," she said in mock disgust, but she was hardly able to contain how it felt to be so wanted after all these years. "You're aware this is sexual blackmail. A felony."

"But you're aiding and abetting."

"A misdemeanor then."

"That I can live with. I'll get the check."

25

"Here we are," Casey said to Kate as his driver pulled up to a mock-Tudor structure on East Sixty-fifth Street between Avenue U and Strickland Avenue in the Mill Basin section of Brooklyn.

"What—no flamingos on the lawn?"

"No, but we can't see the backyard from here."

Kate looked around for her coat, then she remembered she hadn't worn one. It was May weather outside although it was late October, and CNN had said it was going down into the forties in the evening.

She had rarely been to Brooklyn, where Josh had grown up in Bensonhurst. But now, as she stepped out of the car, she experienced how muted the energy in the air was compared to Manhattan.

"Just tell me one thing," she said as they walked up the cement steps guarded by concrete lions. "What do you hope to learn after the madam's already been questioned by three of your gold shields?"

"People tell their stories enough times to enough people, eventually one of those people'll come up with something left out before or maybe hear or see something nobody else did."

She had to agree that Casey's methods worked. He was not a brilliant lawman, but he hung on relentlessly till a clue made itself known.

Over an hour later Casey said to the madam, "Let me get this straight. You never heard of Gregory Haines, even though he came to your house every Friday for years. You also never heard of the Genovese family, even though we have eight-by-tens of you speaking with members this very week. To hear you tell it, you don't have a yellow sheet for being on the pavement and being in the game one way or another for over twenty years."

"Whatever you say," she spat out.

Kate had the distinct sense that the woman in the tailored pink suit and flowing bow tie was dressed more conservatively than usual.

Casey drew closer to his prey, then said in a dramatically sarcastic tone Kate had heard him use with interrogations before, "I suppose, darlin', you can explain how you bought this house for four hundred fifty large when the IRS says you haven't claimed more than twenty-five thou in the past ten years."

"I had a couple great years at the track. What you expect me to do—buy savings bonds?"

Kate smiled despite herself.

"For someone's been around the world more times than Neil Armstrong, you're not talking very smart." His voice hardened. "I expect that after being on the turf as long as you have, you'd know we're not here because we give a dump whether you supply your johns with—with sheep—for Christ's sakes or bend spaghetti with the heads of all Five Families."

He turned from her and paced, hands behind his back. "We wanted to nail you with what we got on you, we'd've been Mirandizing an hour ago." Here the register of his voice lowered conspiratorially and he looked straight at her, appealingly. "We got a serial killer here and we need your help. Please don't make me make your life miserable and—"

"I get it, Casey. I'm not retarded. Absolutely off the record?"

"Absolutely."

Kate admired how he didn't allow his glee to show in his face.

"I'm listening," Casey said. He studied her intently. "Was there anything special on the john's body or on his clothes?"

She remembered the asswipe's voice and words—"or you're furt-erlizer."

An ornate reproduction of an English grandfather clock ticked righteously.

"Nothing. Unless you mean the hard-on he still had," she said, feeling she'd used Solomonic judgment to protect herself.

$\triangledown$

26

"My God," Kate said to Sawyer as she and Josh stood to follow their host into his library, "that was the best Cuban food I've ever had."

"Just some beef with black beans and yellow rice. Greg used to say, 'A potato with friends is a banquet.' God, how he clung to me at times—like seaweed—"

His voice broke like an adolescent's, and Kate and Josh looked at each other, profoundly sad for their host.

They entered the cathedral-ceilinged library of his Gramercy Park brownstone, where a tape of a baroque woodwind quartet was playing on the sound system. The focus of the room, which was filled floor to ceiling with books in rosewood bookshelves, was an early-nineteenth-century umber Japanese screen.

The screen hung above an enormous Chinese daybed accented by an eighteenth-century Turkish tapestry and pillows covered in old Japanese obi fabric. Atop the antique Chinese tables were Ming dynasty equestrian figures. The only illumination in the room came from ginger-jar lamps with parchment shades. The result was elegant until one spotted the anatomically correct male mannequin peeking from behind a potted Rufus palm.

Sawyer looked at himself in the bamboo-framed mirror. He had obviously cut himself shaving around his mustache, and there was a considerable scab under his right nostril that he now monitored as he had all evening by lightly touching it with the pad of his right pinkie.

"God," he said with mock distress, "I look like a raccoon! It's going to take something *heroic* to make me look decent tonight."

Josh was amused. Kate studied his high cheekbones and sharply angled facial planes. What bones he had! There was a russet shadowing around his eyes—makeup? Perhaps it was his reddish brown turtleneck reflecting up into his face.

He took a Dunhill cigarette from a gold case and then looked at them. "Sorry, I know I shouldn't indoors."

"Thanks," they chimed.

"Excuse me," Sawyer said, leaving the room. He returned in moments with a filigreed silver tray containing English tea with scones and clotted cream.

"It was Greg's favorite after-dinner treat," he said, staring down at the cup in front of him as if there was something written on the surface of his tea. "When I went to the morgue to see if it was him, I kept breathing through my teeth, afraid to close my mouth or I'd taste how he smelled."

Kate's eyes stung. Josh remembered when he'd been a medical student and had done the same.

"He was a really good person," Sawyer went on. "Sweet. Decent. Being around him made me want to be better. Made me feel I could. Dead. It's a concept I can't get my mind around. We've—you've got to find whoever—"

"We're doing all we can. Josh, Casey, me, twenty-seven thousand cops twenty-four hours a day, you."

"Me? I'm almost as useless here as a bikini wax to a nun."

Josh laughed heartily and excused himself.

Kate said, "It'll start to heat up for the murderer. It always does. Then he or she'll make a mistake."

"Look at this—we don't even know the sex of the bastard who killed him," Sawyer said despondently. Then he continued in a faraway tone, almost as if they weren't in the room. "I tried a sea change. Took a cruise on the QE II. One day, in a tender in the rain waiting to go ashore, I turned and saw him next to me. Drop-dead exquisite. He had beautiful eyes and teeth, and this style of dressing and caring for his body without being too fussy. The smell of rain and his wet linen shirt came off him . . ."

He paused. It was so quiet in the room Kate heard a piece of ice explode in Josh's drink.

"Suddenly," Sawyer continued, "the engines started up under my feet. I could feel them in every part of my body. Finally, I got up the nerve to speak to him."

The bones of Kate's knees were hard to her hands.

Sawyer said, "The rain stopped, and that afternoon we rode in a car we'd rented on a road that ran into a grove of tropical trees. I can still smell those trees."

Kate moved closer and made an unconscious gesture to reach for Sawyer's hand. Josh placed his paw on her back in agreement.

Without warning Sawyer stopped and pinched the bridge of his nose.

"Well," he began archly, "how do you like the evening so far? If we hurry we can still catch a high mass I arranged at Saint Pat's and then maybe we can go to Temple Emmanuel to hear the Prayer for the Dead."

Josh moved closer to him.

When neither laughed Sawyer said, "Guess I'm afraid one day I'll look into the mirror and see a boring old faggot. That I'll die alone here and no one'll find me till—*Je*-sus—more importantly—*Mary*—will you just *listen* to how she charms new people with her humor and gaiety?"

"Maybe," Kate said, "it would be better if we talked about something else."

"Why was Greg killed?" Sawyer persisted.

Kate said, "The victim is just a person created by the killer."

"What do you mean?" Sawyer said.

"They're not real," Josh said. "The victims. When you have a steak are you eating a steer? Certainly not. You're eating the turf in surf and turf. The victims are toys to him. Body parts."

"Whoa," Kate said, "we don't know this killer is a male."

"C'mon," Josh said, "I never heard of a woman committing a violent, sexually motivated homicide."

"Well, I certainly have." Kate wasn't entirely successful at keeping the irate tone out of her voice. "The assumption that only men commit such murders is too ingrained in male detectives. They automatically exclude any other possibility."

"But—" Josh began.

"I'm not finished. It never occurs to men that something they can't explain at a crime scene might result from a woman's behavior."

"Possible," Josh said.

"I hear you implying, 'Yes, but.' Well, maybe we don't understand what we're seeing at these crime scenes because the killer's not acting and thinking like a man, but like a woman."

"Isn't it true, though," Sawyer said, "that the personality of the serial killer is so well known it's become a cliché? A white man in his thirties, quiet guy next door who's an introvert and collects pornography, has an obsessional fantasy life and deep hidden aggression?"

"You said it," Kate said, "it *is* a cliché. It's nonsense to believe that men and women are at all different in their capacity for murder or lust killing."

"Except," Josh said, "for the different way they're taught to behave."

"But that's learned behavior," Kate countered. "The truth is, women aren't any better or worse than men. We can be just as wicked, just as pitiless, and just as—"

Suddenly the front door chimed and Sawyer excused himself to answer it.

When he returned, Josh and Kate were shocked to see Casey with him.

"Sorry to bother you," Casey said. "You'll probably never tell me your plans for dinner again."

"What is it?" Josh said.

"Another one. This time our friend *schneided* off a souvenir. One guess what it was."

▽

27

CARMINA SAW CANDY, the manager of the phone room, approaching her cubicle. "Yes," she said into her phone, "Daddy's little girl is looking forward to speaking with you again soon, too." She placed the receiver back into its cradle.

Carmina consciously touched her shaved head to make Candy think she was envious of the tangerine hair with black roots piled high on her head Nefertiti-style, which made her spigotlike nose even more noticeable. Hair was not a prerequisite in a phone sex girl.

"Don't tell me," Carmina said, pretending to be annoyed, "Frankie the Freak?"

"Hey, he's become one of our best customers since you started with him last week."

Carmina bluffed: "Can I take him after my break?"

"By then he woulda beat his meat all alone. Next you'll be asking for Blue Cross and personal days off."

"Okay," Carmina pretended to groan.

"Hey, don't do me any favors, Diva. Now put your best tit forward." She turned and shouted behind her: "Okay Fannie, patch her in."

Frankie: H-h-h-hello Diva?
Diva: (whispering) Hi Frankie.
Frankie: Uh-h-h-how are y-y-you?
Diva: Especially wonderful after the last time we spoke sweet stuff. You?
Frankie: A-all right.

Diva: Are you ready for me, Frankie?

Frankie: I th-th-think so.

Diva: Why don't you lay back and put a pillow behind your head? (*Pause.*) That's it. Is your zipper all the way down?

Frankie: Y-yesss.

Diva: Such a good boy. You know what I'm wearing, Frankie?

Frankie: W-w-what?

Diva: My very thin silk black lace bustier across my tits. And on the bottom white stockings all the way up to where my fur ends and a white garter belt and best of all white silk panties. And you know what's covering my crotch?

Frankie: W-what?

Diva: A mesh tongue of silk with a silver strap, Frankie. So all you have to do is open the snap and you can see all my hair.

Frankie: G-g-god. D-d-d-don't forget the h-h-hair s-s-stuff.

Diva: Since you told me how you love my hair I've been letting it grow, so now it's curling out from under my panties. Oh, my nipples are so hard, Frankie. Just like you.

Frankie: Y-y-yes.

Diva: And my pussy—

Frankie: S-s-say the o-o-ther p-p-please.

Diva: My cunt is hot inside now and heavy, like it's being filled up with heated thick oils.

Frankie: M-m-m-more.

Diva: My clit is erect now, just like your cock.

Frankie: Y-y-you know j-j-just—

Diva: Yes baby, I know. Just what you want to hear.

Frankie: Y-y-yes.

Diva: And just what you want to do. God I'm swollen now, and so wet my juices are dripping down slowly into my crack—

Frankie: S-s-say i-i-it.

Diva: My asshole. Oh my God! I just brushed my tit, and now my other hand . . .

Frankie: T-t-tell—

Diva: Sooo soft, like feathers on my thigh. Are you so hard it hurts, Frankie?

Frankie: Y-y-you k-k-know ev-ry—

Diva: Yes, everything you need to hear and imagine and do to me. Oh my, and my cunt is scalding now! I need to come, Frankie.

Frankie: N-n-no please. N-n-not yet.

Diva: I'm stroking her, Frankie, up and down. Back and forth. Now in and out. Oh! Faster and faster. You can't stand it anymore, can you, Frankie? You just want to taste the salt under my arms, the wax in my ears, the dead skin on the bottoms of my tiny feet.

Frankie: Y-y-yes!

Diva: Together now, Frankie. Diva's moving real fast now, pumping her pelvis into her fingers wet and shiny with cunt. It's building. She can't wait. Don't make her wait, Frankie.

Frankie: Oh yes, oh yes.

Diva: Here she comes, Frankie. Frankie now. Oh Frankie! Oh! Oh! Oh! Frankie! Frankie! Frankie!

Frankie: Yesyesyes.

Frankie screamed out with her, a high, plaintive cry that ended in a whimper.

Diva: You know what I'd like Frankie?

Frankie: A-any t-t-thing.

Diva: I'd like you to pull open my snap and get me off in person. Would you like to meet your Diva and see her hairy cunt in the flesh?

The desk clerk at the Abbaye Hotel had them sign in. Carmina signed Aileen Wuornos, the name of the woman

who confessed to killing several men who gave her rides on
Florida highways.

Frankie surprised her with his tall, powerful build and his
clean-cut features. Only the State of Texas–shaped
birthmark on his right cheek kept him from being handsome.

By the time they reached their room little beads of
perspiration had sprung out of the pores in his forehead, his
neck, and the areas above his mouth and beneath his eyes.

She locked the door behind them, then fixed them each a
drink from the miniature liquor bottles on a tray atop a
lowboy.

"Take off your clothes," she commanded, adjusting her
pimento-colored wig.

After he was naked, his well-toned body at odds with his
reticence, she undressed.

While she watched him swallow his digitalis-laced drink
her pulse pounded in her breast.

After they waltzed, she took a condom from her purse and
had him roll it on. Then she lowered herself and rode him
till the digitalis began to work.

When he lay on the floor rocking in pain, she turned up
the music and slid the Ginsu blade out of her purse. With
the thousands and thousands of identical knives that had
been sold through TV, who would be able to trace this one?

With her heart beating in her ears, she climbed on top of
him. He looked up incredulously, too weak now to resist.

She grasped the root of his flaccid member in her hand
and waited a beat to savor the sexual excitement.

Then she thrust the blade down and sawed.

▽

28

THEIR SECOND NIGHT of making love was incredible, better than the first. Perhaps a trifle less passionate but, more important, gentler.

Nina lay in Paul's arms while he slowly ran his fingers through her hair from her forehead to the nape of her neck and then back again.

There had been few moments in her life when she'd experienced such a sense of joy. And never had she liked herself, her own body, as much as this first Sunday morning in November.

The first snowfall last year had filled her with sadness for the death of her flowers and absence of birds in her garden. This snowfall felt indivisible now from the aliveness that heated her almost to a boil and made her skin glow.

"You're a wonderful lover," she said.

"You make giving easy."

"Thank you."

She rolled over and he moved with her, not obediently but trusting, till it was his hair that was stretched out on the pillow. Such a boy's face now with all the tension gone. Sweet. Genuine.

When she looked out her bedroom window everything she saw was as fresh and vigorous as herself: the limb of maple bereft of leaves, the outline of the garage where her father had begun his business, the overhead telephone wires connected to the house, on which the same perched pigeons she had considered flying vermin were now transformed into miniature snowy egrets. Her joy was so strong she couldn't keep from smiling.

"Excuse me," Paul said, sitting up and reaching over to the nightstand for the pitcher of mimosas he had made this morning. He poured them each a cocktail.

"To dreams," he said.

"To you, for making them come true."

She took a sip then kissed the scalloplike scar on his left shoulder. Good God, she thought, is this really what it's like?

"S-so what do you want to do today?" he said.

She was sorry for any return of his stutter but reminded herself how little was left.

"Well, we could go for Caesar salad and pasta at Orazio's and then listen to some jazz."

"That's what we did last—ooh you devil, fooled me again. Wipe that smile!" he added in a parody of anger.

Presently she said, "How about you take a nap and I come back with some fresh coffee beans and bagels and lox and cream cheese from Balducci's—"

"And the Sunday *Times*, of course."

"You said it. I'll make us brunch, and then maybe we can go listen to some jazz at Sweet Basil."

"Basil's sweet? I didn't know. He seems so masculine." Suddenly his expression turned serious. "Christ, I . . . I love you."

The smell of his cologne was on her skin. The taste of his flesh was on her tongue. And both seemed so appropriate. Besides, she thought, watching him rub his temple where a pulse had begun to throb, no one as emotionally vulnerable as him could possibly hurt her. Could this coupling possibly be as right as it felt? Didn't the fact that they were able to speak as old friends say it all? Or was it too soon to speak of love?

She let out a breath she hadn't realized she'd been holding.

"For a long time," she said, "I gave up hope. I feel . . ."

"Yes?"

"Like I've got another chance, with you." She made herself take a breath. "With you it all seems possible."

"It all is. I'll make us brunches on Sundays. And Monday nights you'll make your grandmother's sensational Italian meatloaf."

She wasn't aware that she was smiling because he hadn't stuttered once in three sentences.

"We'll take turns cooking," he went on. "And hurry home every night to be together and talk. We'll travel. Go to museums. Movies. The beach—what's wrong? Are you crying?

"S-s-so h-happy."

"Hey, I'm the stutterer, remember?"

"I remember. You really love me?"

"No, I'm after your family's title."

She smiled. "And here I thought it was my uniform."

His face grew serious.

"I want our baby in your belly."

"Oh Paul," she started.

But her words ended in his mouth.

When their lips came apart she said, "I do love you so. I never thought I'd meet a man like you."

He kissed her palm.

"What's wrong?" he said, having gotten a start from her pulling away.

"Sticking pain in my head all of a sudden."

"Poor baby. Where? Here?"

As he placed his palm on her forehead she recognized how calculated the gesture was. Just as she'd been aware of how insidiously intimate was his kissing of her palm.

"W-what's wrong, Nina? You're shaking."

"Nothing. A chill is all. I must be coming down with the flu or something. Could you be an angel?"

"Anything. Tea? That's it! How's hot tea?"

"Fine, thanks."

As soon as he left the room her head, torso, hands, and feet shrank to childlike proportions. She was small and alone with her father, and it was familiar. She could tell from the tall buildings that they were going to the secret house where she'd get candies from the nice ladies who lived there.

They walked up the stone steps of the house and she smiled, thinking of the candies. When the great big door opened the older lady with the real big bosoms picked her up and swung her. It was fun even though she smelled so strong.

Inside, the other ladies all came out of rooms and made a "big a deal" as Poppa called it. Then Poppa took paper money and folded it up funny in his jacket pocket. The one on top. And went away with one of the ladies to dance to his special song.

She knew Poppa would be back soon. So she ate her candies and watched cartoons on TV.

But then after a while she saw that all the ladies were running around like the canary that got loose in the house once and making funny noises, so she went down the hall to see for herself. When she came to where the ladies were all together outside one door she peeked in the spaces between them and saw her Daddy's arm hanging off a bed.

"Just a second more," she heard a voice say now.

One moment she was in her bedroom waiting for Paul to bring her tea. The next she was watching the ladies pulling her father's clothes back on his stilled body. When his face came into view she saw how pain had twisted his features grotesquely and she screamed.

And then she saw Their horny plates and heard Their grunting and roaring and saw what the torn pieces of color were. A wave of arterial red passed over her eyes.

"Here we are," Paul said, carrying a steaming mug emblazoned with a picture of a hatchet fish.

Nina took the mug with shaking hands, saying, "Please go on with what you were saying about our baby," praying the preciousness of the subject matter would hold the darkness back.

As Paul spoke, her memory of what had happened with her father faded till all she remembered was hurrying up the stone steps eager to taste her candy.

▽

29

Kate glared at her husband as they drove to the morgue from Sawyer Benard's apartment in the gentian-blue Manhattan night.

"What—" Josh said from behind the wheel of their Volvo 850.

"The way you treated me and my opinions in there."

"—are you talking about?"

"You take the cake and the box it came in. First you kept interrupting me, and you know how I hate that, and—"

"But—"

"There you go again."

"Sorry."

"Look, we've talked about all this before—in terms of sexually abused boys. Women abuse the majority. Oral sex, intercourse, some by their own mothers. Teachers, relatives. I even told you about that recent study."

"I do know all this."

"Then you know quite a lot of boys in that study were spanked or submitted to cruelties."

"Yes, so?"

"So, does that sound any different from crimes by men against little girls? Why wouldn't girls be driven to killing, too, because of such treatment?"

"Well, maybe. But surveys are always contradicted. Next week one could come out with the numbers completely reversed."

"All by males, about males. Don't you see? All the

behavioral science analysts at Quantico are men. Just because they say women have never committed sexually motivated murders doesn't make it true."

"Now the Quantico guys are all off base. Right, Kate."

"Yes! How the hell can they be so sure! So many sexual homicides every year are never solved. How can you be so positive none of them are done by women?"

"All I'm saying is there's no record of a female serial killer."

"Because no one's ever proved that a women kill for the same reasons men do. You know that the variables are astronomical when dealing with humans, that presumptions make for inaccuracies. But in every sexual murder case, with no exception, there's the presumption that the murderer is a man."

Josh sighed. "I guess this talk precludes any chance of hanky-panky later on."

"You're a regular Criswell."

"I'll tell you, babe. We keep on like this, one of these days we're gonna get good at it."

"That day is here."

She glared silently at the road.

30

Even at this late hour, Josh noticed, four gurneys were lined up in the receiving area of the morgue, their ghastly burdens waiting to be unloaded into the huge, purring refrigerator.

He walked abreast of Jay Springer and Casey across a reception area to a small room. Springer stopped in front of a long, rectangular plate-glass window beyond which was a gray dumbwaiter shaft. Springer pressed a button beside the window. Immediately a motor hummed, the steel cables moved upward, and the dumbwaiter platform rose, bearing the waxen cadaver of the Widowmaker's latest victim.

For a moment, cut off from the live world above, Josh stood unmoving, waiting for the silence and the isolation of the familiar place to soothe his hurt from the argument with Kate.

"There's a lot of abrasion due to bruxism," Springer was saying. "He ground his teeth. Nervous type."

"Ain't we all," Casey said. "Keep going."

"As you can see he was bulky," Springer went on, "and most of it looks like muscle weight. A meat eater."

Josh took note of the dozens of sunspots staining the cadaver's head, the metastasizing halted by death.

"The mutilization," Jay said, "took place before the victim died."

"Jesus," Casey said.

Josh thought of Kate, who had chosen to wait in the car—still a bit angry at him.

"What do *you* see, Josh?" Springer said.

"What? Oh sorry. What about those hairs you mentioned on the phone?"

"You found *hairs!*" Casey said. "Why didn't somebody tell me?"

Springer said, "Crime Lab should have called you. You know our office is separate from them. We don't usually interact. We work the evidence from the crime scene, they do evidence from the book."

Casey said. "Looks like our buddy is finally tripping. I could get these hairs loaned to you from the Crime Lab, what could you tell from them?"

"That depends," Jay said.

Casey looked at Josh for help.

Josh said, "It depends whether the hairs are from the scalp, pubic area, or armpit, and whether they have root sheaths.

"The hairs that fall out of our heads every day," Josh went on, "are in the last phase of hair growth, the telogen phase. Hairs in this stage have lost their root sheaths, so all you can tell about them is whether they're from a person or an animal, what part of the body they came from, and if they're Negroid or Caucasian."

"And," Casey said, "could you tell the sex of the person if the root sheath was intact?"

"Maybe," Josh said. "You can examine hair for a Y chromosome."

"Correct me if I'm wrong," Casey said. "Only males have Y chromosomes. So you found any Ys, you'd know it was a man?"

"Right," Josh said. "You could use a fluorescent stain and look at the hair under a microscope. Only the Ys would stain."

"So," Casey said, "if it didn't—whatdoyoucallit?"

"Fluoresce," Springer said.

"If it didn't fluoresce," Casey continued, "it would mean it was a woman?"

"Probably," Springer said.

"Probably?" Casey said.

"What about a Barr body?" Josh said to Springer.

"That would do it," Springer said.

"Hey," Casey said, "you guys want me to leave you alone so you can really talk or something? What the fuck's a Barr body?"

"A condensed, inactive X chromosome," Springer said.

"That explains it," Casey said.

Josh bit down a smile. "Females have Barr bodies, males don't."

Casey reached into his back pocket and came out with a piece of white plastic the size of a pack of cigarettes. He flipped it open, pulled up an aerial, punched in a number, and waited.

After a moment he said, "Give me Fasano at the Crime Lab."

A little over two hours later Casey's face was lit with a wide grin.

"You're positive?" he said to the two MEs. "Couldn't it be a woman's hair from a wig?"

"I don't think so," Springer said. "Human hair wigs are pretty rare nowadays. Besides, human hair has flattened cells—scales—all pointing to the tip. If you run your finger along the shaft of a normal human hair, it's smooth one way, rough the other. This is human hair. A woman's pubic hair."

"That *momzer* madam lied to us!" Casey said.

Then Josh slumped so deep in his seat he appeared to be trying to osmose himself into the wood and disappear.

On the way home Josh told Kate what had been discovered.

"I apologize," he said.

"For what—being wrong?"

"For being sexist."

"You got that right."

They drove on in silence for a time.

She remembered having phoned Casey from Bermuda to ask if he'd found any pubic hairs. Evidence at the crime scenes—what little there'd been—had not indicated the sex of the killer. That and her gut had told her it might be a woman.

As they pulled into their driveway he said, "Kiss me. Please."

"Kiss *me*."

When they made love it was urgent and intense, familiar yet novel. They had the patience of old lovers and the passion of new ones.

Afterward she slapped his face softly.

"I really feel awful about how I behaved," he said.

"Good," she said. "Now let's find this broad."

$\triangledown$

31

"**W**HAT DOES IT mean that she took a souvenir this time?" Sawyer said to Kate, Josh, and Jenny as they left their dinner and ambled into the Berman living room. Kate had wanted to return his hospitality, and Jenny had very much wanted to meet him.

"It means," Jenny said, looking nostalgically at the sealed fireplace where flames would now be blazing and applewood scent permeating the room, except that soot was terrible for her illness, "her fantasy has escalated, causing her to make a mistake."

Sawyer said, "The hairs she left behind, which let Josh know the killer is a woman?"

"Precisely," Jenny said.

Kate and Josh smiled, secretly sharing pleasure in how their guest and Jenny were playing Watson and Holmes.

"Does that mean we're close to catching Greg's killer?" Sawyer said. "Just a tear, thanks," he quickly added to Josh, who was pouring brandy for him into a snifter.

"I sure as hell hope so," Josh said.

"Certainly," Kate said, "her self-confidence is what she has most against her. When we learn more about her—and we will—we can take advantage of it. That's plenty, Josh, thanks."

Jenny resumed: "Her cooling-off periods are already briefer. And they'll get even shorter as her fantasy escalates. They'll cause her to get careless again. Make another mistake."

Sawyer took a sip, then watched the brandy glacially melt down the inside of his glass.

Sawyer said, "How much more escalated can our Little Nell get after her last fun adventure?" He raised an eyebrow.

Jenny smiled, snuggling into her favorite place in the room, the padded window seat. "Jerry Brudos, 'The Shoe Fetish Slayer,' had a collection of spiked heels. He'd cut off a victim's feet and jam them into one of his shoes and keep it in his locked freezer. They've kept breasts and nipples in cans, jars of blood. They don't know much really about the opposite sex—as human beings, I mean. So they become curiosity objects for them. They take them apart to see what they're about. They squeeze them and turn them inside out. Taste them."

"Jenny, please," Josh said quickly, seeing how out of focus Sawyer's eyes had become.

"Oh—so sorry," Jenny said, seeing how much of the starch had gone from his shoulders. "I didn't mean—"

"Of course you didn't," Sawyer said.

Kate handed him a glass of ice water. He drank till he was breathless.

"Thanks," he said. "Let's not stop talking about this, please. I have the feeling if I can somehow learn more about . . . this kind of killer I may be able to help. Feel so damn useless."

He turned and looked at himself in a silver-framed mirror on the baby grand piano. His eyebrows ascended comically. "Mary, Mary, I look like I'm about to crawl into a corner and drop six kittens."

No one laughed, although all three found it funny.

Josh stood and poured Sawyer another drink. Despite the cheerfulness of the colors Sawyer wore—rust fatigue sweater layered over a juniper Henley and a buttermilk turtleneck— the darkness in and around his eyes showed how grimly Greg Haines's death was affecting him.

"Thank you," he said to Josh, then turned to Kate. "What do you think?"

"I think Jenny's right. In order to sustain the excitement

our killer'll have to take greater chances or get even more primitive with her fantasy. This need to feed the fantasy overrides self-protective instincts."

Sawyer took a long swallow from his snifter. Refused the cashews Josh offered him from a cut-glass bowl. "What kind of fantasy—revenge?"

"Absolutely," Jenny said. "These are deep needs that can't be satisfied by just kidnapping a man and killing him. This woman's much more complicated. She enjoys watching the tortuous pain an overdose of digitalis causes. She cuts off a victim's penis *before* he's dead. Sadism is the key here. She wants him to know she knows he feels his pain, and that it delights her—"

Josh and Kate looked at each other's faces and found shock that Jenny should know so much about such a depraved subject and pride that she did.

"What makes her do it?" Sawyer said in a voice that contained repulsion and fascination. "An ex-lover or husband?"

"Men throughout her life no doubt exacerbated it," Jenny said. "But it probably started way earlier. Still, there's something here that's an anomaly."

Kate said, "If you give me a minute to bring in the coffee I'd like to hear this."

In the kitchen Josh sliced a carrot cake, then arranged cold fruit in a bowl for Jenny while Kate placed cups of coffee and pitchers of half and half, sugar, and Equal on a black Oriental tray.

"I must say," Kate said, "I wish she'd taken up astronomy as an occupation instead of a vocation."

"She'd still be fascinated by abnormal psychology."

"Aren't you ever wrong?" she said cheerfully.

"Hardly. Nice the way they took to each other."

"Mmm. Poor baby's so lonely, I have to look away. Wish she'd find a boy her own age."

"With her face and shape and mind you have better things to worry about."

Inside Jenny was laughing that eat-out-of-the-can ex-
uberant laugh of hers at something Sawyer had just said.
Her laugh was the most uncomplicated part of her, and Josh
smiled at Kate as if to say, "See?"

"So," Kate said, "what's the anomaly?"

Jenny took a miniature banana from the bowl Josh placed
on a rosewood drum table in front of her. "Most of the time
it's the disorganized killer who keeps trophies. And up to
now this killer has certainly been very organized."

"True," Kate said putting down her fork. "Here I think
the need to live out her fantasy is so compelling her trophy
or souvenir helps her recreate the murder. I think you'll see
more of the same. Worse."

"*Worse?*" Sawyer said. "I couldn't possibly see how,
without the services of a medium."

Everyone laughed.

For a time, no one spoke. There was the friendly sound of
people eating. Then they did some more talking and shared
a few more silences. These last were as communicative as
their conversations.

Suddenly Sawyer dropped his fork onto his dessert plate.
Kate, Josh, and Jenny looked up, startled.

"What if," he said, "the reason Casey hasn't been able to
find the medical source for her digitalis is because it doesn't
come from one?"

Jenny shot a conspiratorial look at Josh and Kate, who
responded with knowing smiles.

"You mean foxglove?" Jenny said.

"Precisely, old bean," Sawyer said, and all three smiled, sure
that he knew that he was only borrowing the role of Holmes
and would soon returned to his confused Watson-self.

Jenny, grinning widely, jumped to her feet and ran and
gave him a high five.

"And you said you felt useless," Josh said.

"Sure," Sawyer said downing the remainder of his brandy.
"Now all we have to look for is a woman who was abused
sexually or verbally, who suffered other disappointments

with men throughout her life, and who now grows foxglove in her window boxes."

"Still," Jenny said, "I can feel the momentum building." She yawned deeply.

"I can tell," Sawyer said.

Jenny yawned again.

"Yawning's a symptom," Josh said. "She's allergic to something here."

"*Well*, thanks a lot!" Sawyer said. "I've certainly been put down before, even in cruising situations. But I've never had *any*one do it *this* directly!"

▽

32

"CHIEF?"

It was Commissioner Ellis.

"I'm on the car phone, Case."

Casey loosened his collar and leaned back in his desk chair. Ellis rarely called him from his car phone and then it was always because he had bad news.

"You heard I've decided to run for mayor?"

"Called your office for congratulations. You were out."

"Sorry I didn't get back to you sooner. I've been away. We got a problem."

Jesus, Mary, and Joseph and the other eighteen saints. There it was.

Casey said nothing, hoping to make it harder.

"What I have to say doesn't have to be bad. I already told you if I win you can name your spot, from commissioner on down."

Casey recognized the sound of ice sloshing in a glass. Ellis rarely drank before sundown. He ran his fingers through his hair, hoping—no, praying—the commissioner wouldn't say what he feared most.

"The Widowmaker case. My advisors—shit! Listen to how I'm talking to you—my *people* say I need this case closed to win."

"It will be closed—soon."

" 'Soon' is too late, amigo. Can't risk it. Got to show the voters I'm prepared to do whatever it takes now—"

"Calling in the fucking Feebies can backfire on you. Your opponent can—and if I know Schecter, he will—say you had to call in the fucking Hoover boys to save the department's ass."

"Hoover's been dead a long time."

"Well, he left a legacy of chicken-shitting that's not to be believed. Don't do this to me, Ellis. Don't let me go out this way."

"My hands are—"

"Then untie them."

"You asked for more people. More than we ever used in a net operation before. Did you get them?"

"Don't ask me questions like that. Know each other too long." Realizing his adversarial tone he added, "I need a little more time, El." Swallowed hard. "Please."

There was a pause. It was the first time he'd ever used that word with Ellis.

Finally the commissioner said, "Seventy-two hours."

"Why don't you just say by fucking sunup?"

"I'd watch it, Casey."

"You're right. Sorry. It's just—"

"I know what it is, and I don't like the arrogant mother-fuckers any better than you. But I'm in the biggest political fight I've ever been in. Make it a week."

Son of a bitch! "I never once asked you before."

"Two weeks. Period. My driver just pulled in. Got to go. Luck, Casey."

Fall down and break your head kissing a baby, you doofus! What a way to go out on the job—the biggest case in your life winding up in the open file.

For a time that would forever remain secret to him, he just sat. His shoulders sank. Then his face seemed to melt, all the resolve leaving it. He looked both younger and older. A middle-aged boy.

He rose and groped to the window. Forced it open and gulped frigid draughts of air till he shook with cold. When he slammed it closed, he had not a molecule of doubt where he was heading.

He grabbed his hat from the rack. Then he remembered his driver. Pressed the intercom button.

"Lenore, tell Jim to take the rest of the day off."

▽

33

CARMINA SAW DOMINIQUE, the manager of the Fantasy Escort Service, approaching the burgundy chintz couch on which she sat doodling a convulsed man on a *Penthouse* centerfold.

The two other women on the couch were watching a commercial on TV in which a stain peeled off a boy's shirt and tap-danced after being washed in a blue granulated detergent.

"You're up, Diana," Dominique said, pointing a rodlike finger whose nail was enameled neon green at Carmina.

Dominique had a mane of several shades of blond ranging from ash to medium brown. Her darting eyes were the color of mercury and emitted a wild menace barely held in check.

As Carmina stood, Cleo, a Crayola redhead from Brooklyn whose real name was Mabel, stopped her gum chewing long enough to sing in a mock stage voice: "She's just a girl who cain't say no—"

"Enough of that bullshit." Dominique's eyes stabbed Cleo, who cowered exaggeratedly in her chartreuse Spandex top.

Jezebel, the other woman on the couch, looked on with the same tragic light in her gray eyes Carmina had noticed since her own arrival a week ago.

"Hey," Cleo said to Dominique, "whaddaya call someone's always there before time?"

"Okay, okay, I give up," Dominique said, arms akimbo.

"A premature ejaculator," Cleo said.

Dominique rolled her eyes. Carmina concentrated on the feeling below her navel. It was as if her blood had warmed and thickened. She knew this one would be her Next.

Carmina followed Dominique, smoothing down her swimming-pool-green metal-studded dress by Giorgio di Sant'Angelo. Clinique's bronzing gel made her skin appear as if she were an octoroon or, as Dominique put it, "a high yellow." This was italicized by her dusky hair, which had been styled into long cornrows, each little pigtail clipped at the end with a barrette in the shape of a miniature bar of gold bullion. Her contacts were a shade like the inside of a kiwi.

In Dominique's office, burgundy furniture stood on a pink shag rug. Dominique sat behind the pink faux-marble desk and handed Carmina a pink index card.

"His name is Earl Washington. He's staying at the Pierre, but you got to meet him in this new restaurant Veronica's Vase on Fifty-seventh and Eighth. The address is on the card. Eight sharp. Here's twenty for cabs, and don't forget the receipts this time."

Carmina rose.

"One other thing," Dominique said. "He said he wasn't interested in anything but company. His wife died not long ago. Anyway, that's what he said. But he said it three times. Oh, and he's also black."

"Well now, Miss Scarlet, I finally git to be myselves."

"What are you—the new Cleo? You better get going."

Carmina retrieved her new leopard-skin coat, Ray-Bans, and Bottega Veneta briefcase, in which she carried the Ginsu blade—a symbol of order to her. This time she also jammed in two Ziploc bags.

At the door Cleo called after her: "Just think of yourself as one of Fantasy Escort Service's Joanie Appleseeds of pleasure."

When Carmina stepped out of the taxi, a flock of pigeons rose and burst up against the sky. There was the smell of burning chestnuts mixed with carbon monoxide.

The feeling below her navel had intensified despite her having masturbated in the taxi. And last night she had masturbated picturing her last victim's face contort and turn purple. She had orgasmed with the knowledge that he knew it was she who was killing him. That hers was the last face, the last of anything, that he saw before he died.

At Veronica's Vase a maitre d' led her past people-sized black glazed vases out of which sprang enormous sprays of pussy willows to a gray leather banquette on which was a miniature vase filled with pussy-willow buds.

Earl Washington was so large he stood in sections when she arrived at his table. When he smiled, gold winked at her and his skin appeared to crack in spots like dried chocolate pudding.

He had a high, receding forehead and sparse yet tight ridges of hair. The ridges looked like divots of black earth on his walnut head. He smiled with his milky-lime eyes as well as his large lips.

She removed her Ray-Bans and stung him with her look. Then she licked her lips and gave him a lewd smile. Big as he was, he came round to pull out her chair with a slow and light gracefulness.

She ordered a Stoli Cristall martini.

"Absent friends," he said, lifting his Grand-Dad old-fashioned, his eyes misty.

She pretended to yawn, extending her arms overhead, letting the movement draw her breasts into relief against the front of her dress.

He didn't respond. Still, she got an incendiary thrill thinking of just how close to peril he really was.

"I hope you'll excuse me . . ." he said. "I just lost my wife—not very long ago . . . I'm so nervous I can't even read the menu. You're a beautiful woman and so young, and I'm . . . I'm completely at a loss what to say—"

"It's my nature to please men, especially kind men who've lived with and need to be succored by a woman. I'm a stranger who can't hurt you. Say whatever comes into your mind. In time the hurt will find its way out with the words. The drinks and the food will help, too." Here she dropped her voice to below a whisper. "And later we'll listen to some special music I brought and I'll show you how relaxed I can really get you." She watched him look up and into the crosshairs of one of her most innuendo-filled smiles.

"Please don't misunderstand, but I already told the woman at—where you work—that all I wanted was companionship. My wife hasn't been gone very . . . I never meant . . ."

She fixed her eyes on his defiantly. "Never's a long time. Why don't you just tell me things. All the things that you think to say."

She tolerated his knock-knock jokes. And acted absorbed when he droned on about how much he had loved his departed saint of a wife.

"Jesus God," he said after a while, "it seems I forgot your name."

"Diana."

"Riiight. Pretty."

"It means protector of slaves."

"Too bad you didn't know my great gran'folks."

"And mine," she said, thinking: Diana also means huntress.

She ordered a caviar cannelloni appetizer and the filet mignon with chèvre and quail-stock sauce for an entrée. If he actually insisted they restrict their time to companionship, at least she would have stung his wallet.

He ate little of his peanut butter soup or his red snapper with violets and pine nuts. Instead he talked about his wife's simple but delicious cooking. How they'd met marching on Washington with Reverend Martin Luther King.

Her strategy was to keep ordering drinks in the hope that eventually the alcohol would free his long-dormant libido.

Finally, after their second after-dinner stinger, she saw his eyes fasten on her risen breasts as she stretched.

"Want something," she said, "or just looking?"

"Sorry . . ."

"Don't be. I'm not. I was beginning to feel invisible." She made a smile work its way to her lips. "C'mon, give a girl a break and ask her to dance."

She let him lead her to the tiny dance floor in the rear, where she clutched him tightly and used her belly strategically.

Before long she could feel him harden against her thighs.

She whispered in his ear, "I'd like to know what makes you twitch, Earl Washington. I never feel I really know a man till I find out what it takes to make him scream out in bed."

"God have mercy," he said breathlessly.

As they danced naked on the ivory carpet in his hotel room she looked down and mused, "Stands out like a nigger on an iceberg."

"Hey—" he said dreamily, "what's a black gal doing carrying around some Eyetalian's music with her?"

"What are you—part of the Black Inquisition?" She kissed his lips, which were as cushiony as the Mason Dots her motherfucking father had fed her as a girl in the movies.

Then she stood back and burned him with a look.

In bed she looked up from between his legs and grew wet when she saw the way his mouth was twisted with desire—a preview of how his whole being would soon be spasmed in pain. She fingered herself then, and a smile parted her lips as she rubbed her fingers over his mouth and lips and tongue.

She pulled the condom over his engorged cock and mounted it as he grunted and moaned.

She realized he had already come as he literally wilted out of her.

"Sorry . . ." he said, panting. "Long time—good God, my heart!"

The news that the digitalis had begun to work brought her almost instantly to orgasm.

Later, Earl had rocked on the floor and struggled to stay alive more than Carmina would've guessed, given how much he missed his wife. Which proved he would've soon found another wife to be unfaithful to.

She went over to see if the old black bastard was faking it. He was dead, all right.

She retrieved her briefcase and took out the Ginsu blade.

When she cut out his black heart, a dark porridge spilled onto the rug.

She placed the still-warm heart in her purse in the doubled-up, self-sealing Ziploc. Then she cleaned herself and any traces of herself.

At the door she turned and said, "Have a holly jolly Christmas."

Hours later in her bedroom she was patting bathwater from her body when the pork-roast smell of flesh and blood cooking wafted from the kitchen.

She hurried barefoot into the kitchen and forked her dinner onto a Limoges plate.

Then with her Ginsu she cut a piece of meat, rolled it around in blood, and, eyes boiling over, ate.

▽

34

"HERE'S HEALTH TO your enemies' enemies," Casey said under his breath to Ellis.

He was in Sean's, a sound enough saloon by today's standards, with dark wood, a brass rail, and an old-fashioned tile floor. But it didn't even resemble Devon's, the bar his father had owned on the same site way back. Back when his stomach was still hard and when you said drugs people thought you meant penicillin and a toy stamped MADE IN JAPAN meant it was cheap and would break with any use.

Now the sound of music startled him and he looked up. On the back bar TV Michael Jackson was peeking at him through the fingers of a white glove. Casey raised his hand for the bartender, a boy in his early twenties whose large ears and overbite gave him a rabbitlike appearance.

"Here's a little something for your cup, Johnny, if you'd be kind enough to get that whatever-he-is out of my sight." He slipped him a ten.

The young man hit the off button with the remote and poured another, and Casey drank it. The whiskey had more of a kick after his lay-off. And he certainly hadn't lost his taste for it.

His father had run Devon's like a public house/bank/club. Regulars received cards, cakes, and presents every birthday. The wood glowed (at seventy-five feet, it was the longest bar in Manhattan). The ice was kept in bags in the freezer to retain its hardness, as in the fancier uptown hotel bars. There were no measuring gizmos on the bottles.

If a man went to the john, his date was protected by the
bartender. No novice actors or dancers, Devon's bartenders
were ex-officers in the IRA. They could relieve hangovers and
stop hiccups.

Jimmy Breslin might have called Devon's "a good, drinking bar." It was the kind of place that could cure a headache.

Now he let the bartender tell him what was the matter
with the Giants this year. The boy was so pale he might have
lived all his life in a tavern.

Casey could have gone to one of the bars where cops hung
out. But he knew his loneliness would be even worse. When
he was just a uniform, he'd had more cop buddies than he
could count. But as he'd climbed upward in the department
it became lonelier and lonelier. The hell with these depresso
thoughts! He was going to drink as much as he fucking well
felt like.

The whiskey went down nice and easy. But soon a vapor was
rising behind his eyes, unfocusing them. And the floor had
begun to give way underneath him. He climbed on a stool.

The baby of a bartender returned, and Casey tried to
explain how and why Feebies weren't like they were in the
days when guys like Efrem Zimbalist, Jr. played them, how
they'd gotten as crooked as the CIA, how as an American
he was ashamed of them. Besides, instead of cooperating
with local law enforcement they tried to order you around.

The bartender frowned, confused and irritated. Casey
knew he was making wonderful sense and couldn't understand why the meaning of his words was being lost on the
boy, who seemed bright enough.

"I don't know what you mean," the bartender said. "Who
are the Feebies? Hey, please, no more to drink, huh buddy?
You don't want to get me in trouble, do you?"

Hadn't Casey already explained? His thoughts, at least to
himself, were crystal clear.

"Crystal," he said.

It was then that the bile born of the earlier conversation
with Ellis rose in him.

He made his way on a floor that kept moving to the men's room, where he lost his lunch and the meal before that.

The act sobered him a little, and he washed his face in the mirror. In the ruthless fluorescent light all his weariness and defeat showed. Sixty-three years of accumulated scars and nicks and sags. He thought of the promise he'd made to Kate and Josh and had to look away from his reflection.

He apologized to the bartender for the mess he'd made in the bathroom and left a twenty-dollar tip. Then he left, trying to adopt a gait that wouldn't mark him as a victim.

After he had gotten no more than a few steps outside Sean's he saw, with peripheral vision, movement in a shadowy doorway to his right.

"All your money *now!*"

Casey saw the blade. It was a push-button half a foot long. Holding the knife was a boy of twenty, tops. Even in the shadows Casey could see his acne-pitted cheeks.

"Take it easy, fella. You can have all the money I got."

Casey reached inside his jacket pocket then suddenly dropped his shoulder, pivoted on his heel, and struck the boy's wrist with his other foot. The knife went up in the air. When the boy went for the blade he was off balance and Casey got a hand on him, spun him round, and caught him with a right hand square in the nose. The boy cursed him.

Just before the blow came Casey saw the boy's eyes change and his lips draw into a smile. Brass knuckles of all things. He saw the knuckles through a pale yellow vapor as he whirled around to face the boy, the light failing, his eyelids closing down.

"Now you're gonna get yours, old man," the boy said, his voice growing more distant. A bad connection getting more staticky.

The boy's features were in front of his then, an insane grimace on his mouth, his eyes wild in his waxy face. Casey's sphincter tightened. Then he pulled, dragged himself up from unconsciousness, and swung a blind fist that struck insignificantly on the boy's arm. The boy jumped onto his back, got his forearm under Casey's chin hard against his throat. Before Casey could pull it off, the boy'd locked it into the crook of his other arm. All things from a mugger he'd never expected a police stranglehold.

The boy pushed Casey's head forward against the back of his forearm, thrashing the air from him. Casey elbowed at his ribs but the boy had his head pressed so far forward that little lights began to appear in front of his eyes. And he began a slow slide into blackness.

In what he believed was his final hope, Casey threw himself backward with all his might. Carrying the boy, he came down on top of him. Somehow the boy squirmed away and Casey struck his tailbone against the curb. A numbness ran down both legs.

The boy was on him again, nearly accomplishing another stranglehold, when from his old Marine training Casey instinctively hooked his thumb behind a strand of tendons in the boy's upper arm.

The boy yelped.

"Got to know the entry point," he heard his drill instructor say, "or you'll break your thumb."

The boy fell to his knees, then on his back. Casey threw a left to his nose. Then let loose his thumb and brought all of his weight into the right that followed.

Then another. And another. Blood gushed from the boy's nose and mouth.

Casey, panting, stopped himself.

Then pulled out his cellular phone and punched in nine-one-one.

"This is Chief Casey. I'm on"—he looked for a street sign but didn't see one—"a few steps from Sean's bar on Lexington. Number eighty-something. Send a blue-and-white and—"

The mugger made a motion to rise, and Casey readied his fist. But the boy slumped down on the pavement.

$\triangledown$

35

CASEY WOKE AND saw Nora standing close by. She softened the way she held her head and kissed him, beginning a different state of awareness for him in which there was no light, not even feeling, except where their lips and tongues touched. Her hand slid between his legs, finding hollows and corners no others had found.

Nora rose and squatted over him, took hold and guided herself carefully down the length of him.

But by the fourth time she rose his resolve had begun to recede. She climbed off and strode to the bathroom.

"Sorry," he said when she'd returned, "it's—"

"I know what it is."

He was alarmed at all the pain he saw in her face. Even the warm amber whiskey color of her eyes had turned cold and dark.

"Jesus. It's not like I've been hitting it every day, is it?"

"No, but you damn well want it every day."

"Seems to me that's quite a difference."

Suddenly her eyes brimmed over and she wept.

He rose from the bed, feeling the pain in his hands as he pushed off. His knuckles were skinned, his palms ringing. Moving, he became aware of how weak he was. His neck and throat were sore and his tailbone ached. There was a clot of blood in the iris of his left eye.

She had collapsed in a chair and he cuddled her, feeling foolish about feeling foolish to be cuddling her when he was naked, but knowing it wasn't right for him to get his robe from the closet.

"I'm sorry," he said, "I'll be okay in a little while. You know I want you, darlin'."

"Told you it's not that. It's been killing me to watch you every day needing a drink. I even went to a few Al-Anon meetings."

He drew back, unbelieving.

"I figured they could help me deal with you."

"I really think you're overreacting here."

She pulled out of his arms, her eyes red with tears and anger.

"Do you?" she said sarcastically.

She closed her eyes, and when she opened them said, "I love you more than I've ever loved any person. But if you don't try to help yourself change I'm going to leave before you wreck my life along with yours."

He didn't—it felt like he couldn't—answer, silenced by all the feelings of shock, indignation, fear, compassion, and self-loathing that struck him at once.

▽

36

"JUST FIVE MORE minutes," Paul called to Nina from the kitchen. It was Christmas Eve and he had insisted he make them dinner. Nina's surprise would be that he'd made them a seafood meal similar to the ones she'd told him had been traditional in her family the night before Christmas.

As he lit the bayberry candles in the dining room, he noticed that Nina's wineglass had a hairline crack. Damn! It was too late to buy another with dinner almost ready, so he switched his glass with hers.

"What is it smells so scrumptious?" Nina called out.

"That's you, silly. Your new perfume."

"Seriously, can't I help?"

"You could put on some nice dinner music while I open the wine."

"What are we having, red or white?"

He started to say white but caught himself. "Nice try. But you'll just have to wait to see what surprise I cooked."

He checked the garlic toast she'd described that her father had made that one special night a year. Perfect! Carefully, so as not to break any, he set the toast into one of his sister's breadbaskets in which he had placed a dinner towel with a pattern of tiny Christmas trees he'd bought last week for this evening. Gingerly he folded the towel over the toasts to keep the heat in.

Two minutes, three at the most, and dinner would be ready.

Nina sat on the couch with her feet tucked under her,

admiring the tree they had decorated together. What kind of an Italian woman did he think she was, assuming that she wouldn't recognize the smell of shrimps and lobster and scallops cooking, not to mention, God bless him, *baccala*. But she wouldn't ruin his surprise if someone threatened to tear all her nails out. There could never be another man as thoughtful, as gentle, as sweet as her Paul.

Suddenly the smell of garlic toast wafted out to her nostrils and her thoughts spooled back to the first Christmas after Poppa had died.

She had sat at the great white island of a dining room table her mother and her mother's family had filled with fishes and bread and pasta dishes. Funny, she had thought, how none of Poppa's sisters and brothers were there.

"A *schivazzo* is what he was," she heard her aunt Carmella say. Then saw her mother cry.

Nina cried now with her mother again for the millionth time since Poppa died in the house Mama called *puta's casa*.

"Don't cry for a *disgracia*," her uncle Fredo said to her mother.

And then she remembered how her mother had had the great cement vat taken down, and men in trucks anesthetized Them and then lifted Them out and hauled Them away. How long afterward she and her mother had still smelled the invasive odor, worse than dead rats. Her mother had hired men who spread lime, and the smell went away. But sometimes, like now, memory still carried it, like offal held to her face.

Now her body was trembling. But hard as she fought the memory, it came sharper and sharper into focus. And soon she was sitting on the floor in her room playing with her Chatty Cathy dolly and she looked up and Poppa was there in the doorway. She smiled but then she saw that his eyes had changed and looked like the oil that came out of his car when the man in the gas station made it go up on the thing he called a "lift." Now she saw his penis sticking out of the front of him like some out-of-place bent finger and then growing, like toys in cartoons that came alive at night. And she knew.

"Come, little one," Poppa said like he always did when he was going to do things to her down *there*, so she cried and begged him. But that didn't help because he wasn't Poppa anymore.

She wet herself when he touched her and he yelled in the voice, like thunder and lightning, that he got with the oil eyes.

She kicked and scratched as he carried her out to the garage where They lived. She was shaking all over and couldn't breathe. In her mouth was the taste of a roller-skate key. He took a dog from one of the cages holding the cats and dogs he got at the pound. Then he dragged her up to the big house They lived in made of sidewalk and then up the metal ladder.

There were three of Them, crocodiles just like in Tarzan pictures, long and fat as trees. Their house wasn't big enough for Them and They lay half on, half off each other. But now They smelled food and started to go *hiss*—and *ungh, ungh, ungh*—and then roar. The dog barked and showed its teeth as the man who used to be Poppa threw it down on top of the three of Them. The dog hit the water, swam to a log and shook itself.

"WATCH," the man who wasn't Poppa said, and held her head so she would. Suddenly, the biggest of Them, as long as a telephone pole, grabbed one of the dog's legs with his great big head and then crashed it against the log. Nina screamed and squeezed her eyes shut, but she could still hear a howl and then the terrible sound of the dog's skin exploding against the bone. She squeezed her eyes even tighter but the sound of the splashing was just as bad as seeing. When finally she opened her eyes the dog's hind legs were sticking out of two of Their mouths.

"PleasePoppapleaseplease I'll be good! I'll do anything you want! Pleeease—"

But still he tore off her clothes from her little body and then tied her to a chair and lowered her down toward Them.

"I will teach you to listen to your Poppa!" he screamed.

They were all three snapping Their giant heads in the water and making noises as loud as airplanes.

Despite herself Nina looked down at Them. All three were jumping up straight out of the water. She could see Their slit-shaped yellow eyes, each jaw carrying a row of teeth bigger than her fingers and more than she could count. One of Their scales cut the bottom of her right foot.

Suddenly she felt a balloon of red color bubble and push its way out of her heart and up into her head. Then heard a sound behind her eyes like Mama made when she tore old shirts into rags. Little Nina looked down at one of Them as its mouth barely missed her bleeding foot. She looked but didn't see.

Her body was rocklike.

But her mind had escaped and was safe. Free.

Now Nina hurried to the bathroom, flushed the toilet, and vomited. Then she laved her face and neck with cold water again and again as if she could somehow wash the memory out of her head. The water turned so cold it left her breathless. Still the memory persisted. One doesn't have to die to go to hell, she thought.

When Nina left the bathroom she saw Paul's arm extended toward her like a question.

"Dinner is served," he said as he led her to the table. "You okay, sweetheart?"

"Fine," she said, and worked her lips into a smile. But she had detected another calculated gesture by him. And look at the amaryllis he purposely used as a centerpiece because he knew it was her favorite! And the bayberry candles, which she'd told him Mama always used Christmas Eve—what kind of trick was in his head?

"It's . . . overwhelming. I love everything!" another part of her said, looking at the table setting.

She tried to calm herself by buttering her garlic toast, talking about the tree, and filling Paul's salad bowl and her own with radicchio and arugula—a mantra of the ordinary she hoped would soothe the part of her that was convinced that any instant the single frayed filament by which she knew herself and existed would snap.

"Oh my God," she enthused as he carried in platter after platter of seafood. "You remembered." Yes, she thought, and how else are you planning to deceive and betray me?

She pressed her hands down on the table till the new tremor was barely visible.

A white china bowl appeared in front of her face.

"Calamari salad," Paul said.

"Minute. Thanks."

Hard as she tried to believe in his smile, to keep a trust she knew somehow was connected with the fine strand that was her life, she couldn't. Everything he said rang a half-note off sincere.

Some obscure, nascent power as undaunted as gravity began to overtake her. Her heart was pounding so hard she thought her ears would explode and shoot out a stream of blood. Blessed Mary and all the saints, help please!

But hard as she held on, she felt herself rise out of her head, rise to the absolute edge of herself, then explode and scatter.

"Are you all right, Nina?"

A man's voice came to her as if from across a great body of water.

When her eyes focused she saw that it was Nina's boyfriend. What kind of fool did he take her for, pretending with his pinched face to be so concerned? Maybe, like all men, he betrayed so naturally he didn't even know he was doing it.

She'd never trusted him. It was all she could do at the moment to keep from reaching out and stabbing her nails into his deceitful eyes.

Instead she said in a Ninalike tone, "Went down the wrong pipe. I'm fine, honey."

"Maybe this big a dinner wasn't such a good idea."

"It was the sweetest thing anybody ever did for me. Just that something didn't go well with the puttanesca sauce."

"Try the Bolognese."

"I will. Would you mind getting me a little water?"

"Right. Sure I mind."

When he was out of sight, she reached into her pocket. Retrieving the sterling pillbox she'd stuck in there this morning knowing the lovesick bitch wouldn't notice, she emptied the powder into his glass of Frascati. "Try that," she whispered.

He returned, and after she'd drunk a respectable amount of water she said, "Do you mind if I put on some music?"

"Please."

After she'd put the tape into the player, she felt the blood thicken under her navel.

"What's that you're playing?" he said when she'd returned to her seat.

"It's the very last music my father heard."

Eyes shining with love, he took her hand. Turning it over, he kissed her palm.

▽

37

As soon as Josh opened his front door and saw Jenny's face, he knew something was wrong.

"You've been eating Raisinets. I thought you promised Aunt Kate you'd lose weight," she said once they had embraced.

"Damn! I had one lousy Raisinet hours ago. What's wrong? It seems far from a Merry Christmas for you." He took her overnight duffel and they went inside arm-in-arm.

"I broke up with a man."

"I'm sorry, honey."

"Thanks."

She went immediately to stand with her rear to the fireplace he and Kate had had sealed off because of her illness, as though her body had remembered where she could best warm it fast.

"Can I get you something?" he said.

"Thanks, no. I'm feeling way off. Where's Aunt Kate?"

"She went to pick up some pies Betty Ebling baked for us. Here, lie down on the couch. I'll turn up the heat. Be right back."

She watched him lumber out of the room, thinking of his ability to transform problems into opportunities. Her aunt Kate had turned the traumas in her early life—such as her father's getting shot and killed on duty—into the ability to excel. Josh used his pain to keep him balanced through the stormiest of times.

He acted on problems immediately. Her aunt tended to store problems—she simply was not in as much a hurry to resolve them as Josh.

These differences usually led Jenny to seek solace from him. Being with him was like being away from herself.

Josh returned saying, "So. Talk. Please. I'm listening."

"I miss him so—the way he'd cant his head sometimes when we were intimate—and when he kissed me the first time we were in a taxi, and he's ruined taxis for me forever. I can't stand the pain, not the way I've been feeling physically . . . Oh, who's going to love someone as sick as me, Uncle Josh?" Her face collapsed and she wept.

Josh felt a sort of visceral lurch as he recollected a lost love from his youth. Something settled lower within him, then shriveled. He went over and took her in his arms, and she soaked the shoulder of his shirt with tears. He rocked her as he'd done when she was a child. Then too she had often worn that same helpless look, that maddening expression of low self-esteem. Then it had been for her mother and father's having died. Now it was for a young man who she assumed would not have left her if she were well.

Josh hated that plaintive look of hers, her yielding, apologetic voice. He found himself wanting to urge, even scold, her.

He excused himself and returned with two fingers of brandy in a jelly jar.

"Hey," she said, "that's my old Flintstone jelly glass."

"Yabba-dabba-do."

When she laughed, a relief tidal in scope washed over him.

He said, "All the brandy glasses are being washed in the dishwasher for tonight. Jen, I lost both my parents and my brother in that one most terrible day of my life. You know I had a breakdown about that time. I never told you that the breakdown had already started weeks before."

Watching the absorbed look in her eyes, he was grateful to get her mind on something other than her own problem.

"I looked at myself then as what the shrinks now call a 'deficit model.' I was drop-dead in love with a cheerleader. We were both needy kids. My parents were reserved. Hers were divorced and always competing against each other to win her love. One day she dumped me."

"Poor Uncle Josh."

"Absolutely. 'Woe is me' became my mantra. The United Jewish Appeal found me a free shrink. He taught me that when someone's been playing Hamlet all his life it's not easy to learn light comedy."

"Meaning?"

"I felt that because I hadn't gotten affection as a kid my life was a big drama. I believed—and it was like a drug—that my pain was more significant than other people's. Poor special little me."

Jenny laughed and hugged him till her bones hurt his.

She said, "You've known for a while I was having trouble with a man, didn't you?"

"You didn't mention one word about anything masculine in Buffalo. A person who's happy about men doesn't usually avoid the subject."

"I didn't throw you off with my fierce focus on the Widowmaker, huh? I feel so—transparent."

"We're all glass sometimes. You know what? I think it's time you learned to let your own light shine."

"How did you pull yourself together that time over that cheerleader?"

"By dragging myself to that shrink—hey, here's your aunt Kate."

Kate saw at once that Jenny had been crying.

Jenny explained all they had talked about.

Kate hugged her and said, "It's a good idea to get more serious about handling your emotions. A bad thought is like inhaling a toxic chemical or eating a food you're allergic to. The mind can make amazing changes in the body. I read of a case of multiple personality in which one personality was so allergic to peanuts it could have died from just one, while another could eat an entire pound without any effect. Learning to deal with your emotions better can save your life."

"Yes, ma'am."

"I didn't mean to preach."

"If you guys can't preach to me, who can?"

▽

38

CHRISTMAS MORNING CASEY pulled himself up from the plaid La-Z-Boy in Nora's den. The smell of bacon and coffee pulled him away from the TV screen, on which a Budweiser commercial had interrupted the scene in *Red River* where John Wayne and Montgomery Clift fight and make up.

Nora stood over a huge black skillet in a quilted pink robe—one of the gifts he had given her last night. His eyes sought and found the gold claddagh ring with an emerald held by two hands he had given her for their engagement four days ago. He didn't smile, but his eyes lit, seeing the Gaelic symbol of their love.

He looked at the bank calendar depicting Santa Claus and was reminded that he had only six days left to catch the Widowmaker before Ellis called in the Feebies.

Suddenly he needed a drink. He wanted one to stop what he was feeling. Instead he leaned over the skillet and inhaled the glorious smell of hand-cut cottage fries crisping, as if it could immunize him against his thirst.

She turned the burner off the stove, dished out the food, and set down the plates on the Formica table. Silently he set out the tableware and napkins. She took off her apron, put out her arms to him, and beseeched him with her eyes. He drew her close, and she hugged her fiercely.

The ultimatum she had given at the end of their last fight had changed him fast and forever. No way was he going to lose this best of women, this friend, to anything at all, even whiskey.

After the meal as always, they ignored the dishwasher, which both agreed didn't do as thorough a job. She washed and he dried.

"Six more days," he said absently as they finished off the knives and forks.

"Something'll come up. It's bound to."

"Goddamned Ellis, two weeks he gives me, like catching the Widowmaker is the same as filling out some cockamamy report on serial murderers. Now to put the cherry on the cake she's gone and done a black. As if we didn't have enough trouble coming up with a profile before. And she's gotten so meshuga she took another souvenir. We got as much chance of catching her in six days as . . . as the Pope has praying in Swahili."

He lit a cigarette. Crushed it out immediately.

"You don't even have to light these Camels," he said, "to get cancer. Just holding them's enough. Eight years without a cigarette, and now—"

She didn't say anything, and they let the silence continue.

A few moments before noon he phoned the AA Intergroup number and told the volunteer who answered that he needed an evening meeting in or near Rhinebeck "just in case."

"It's a good man I've promised myself to," she said in her exaggerated brogue. "Maybe when we get to Josh and Kate's we'll hear of something new they've come up with about the case."

"On Christmas day, with Jenny there and that Sawyer feller, or whatever he is?"

"Kate did say she has a surprise for us."

After Christmas dinner Kate stood and said, "Now, a little surprise." Casey watched, squirreling in his seat.

Josh handed Kate a silver-wrapped package, and she handed it to Nora.

Nora opened the package and held up a framed watercolor.

"The prettiest painting of Galway Bay I've ever seen. Thank you so much." She looked over at Casey, who sputtered, "Oh . . . very grand . . . grand . . ." She knew he was disappointed that the surprise had nothing to do with the Widowmaker.

Nora looked up to find another wrapped box in her hands. It was from Sawyer. She removed a burlap sack inside of which was a many-eyed Waterford crystal potato. "Well I never," she said, laughing. The rest joined her.

Next Jenny handed Casey a tiny box that contained a glass pig blown in Dublin.

Over some cherry and mince pie, hot chestnuts, and fresh ground coffee, Casey was able to smile enough to encourage Nora. Jenny worried Josh and Kate by desperately trying to have fun. Sawyer got drunk and began maneuvering around the room showing photographs of himself and Greg Haines on vacation in Saint Bart's.

After he spilled an entire snifter of brandy on his turtleneck, Sawyer refused Josh's offer of another shirt. "This umber color was Greg's favorite," he said in a determined voice. "I won't change it."

Before long Jenny got a migraine, which confused Josh and Kate—everyone had been so careful about not wearing perfume or aftershave, and they'd all worn only natural fibers.

Jenny blamed her headache on the smell of lily of the valley, to which she was allergic. But no one was wearing it. Kate said one of them must have picked up the scent from someone before arriving and carried it in on their clothing. None of them could detect the odor.

Sawyer passed out as soon as he came in contact with the bed in the guest room. Jenny fell asleep on the couch. Kate and Josh walked Nora and Casey to their car. Then all four exchanged kisses.

Kate looked into Casey's face and tenderly pushed back a lock of silver hair from his eyes.

"I know, darlin'," she said, "only five more days. We'll get her."

▽

39

AT 2:43 A.M. Kate came suddenly awake. She was tired and irritable from lack of rest. But when she tried to clear her mind for sleep something nagged at her.

She had learned long ago that there was little on earth to compare with that unique hell of trying to sleep. She looked over at Josh, and her lips shaped into a smile. How often she wished she were blessed with his gift of being able to use sleep as a refuge when troubled.

She pulled herself off the bed carefully so as not to disturb him, put on a robe, and padded downstairs, where she used the bathroom. Then she went to the kitchen, boiled water, and steeped two spearmint tea bags in a pot, leaving out her usual teaspoon ration of honey for fear the sugar might keep her awake.

"Now," she said, "what woke me?" Talking to herself aloud sometimes helped her turn the unprocessed data that formed her hunches into facts.

Often she imagined she could hear her father's voice. Now it was saying: "You feel the solution to the case is just floating out there. So close you can touch it. But you can't quite get there yet."

"Any ideas, Pop?"

"Stop analyzing. Use your fine Irish gut. Listen to your vibes, like the kids say. Feel the pictures in your mind."

"Wait. Where are you going?"

"For a haircut. And then the ball game. Then I thought I'd stop by the tavern and hoist a few brews and balls with the guys. Now where would a dead detective be going? Merry Christmas, darlin'. Only four days left before the Feebies."

"Don't remind me."

And he was gone.

"Feel the pictures in your mind." She smiled, remembering how he'd known that, decades before the technique of visualization became popular.

She took her tea in the living room, where she sat on the couch. Closing her eyes, she tried to call up the images that had awakened her.

Nothing. Her eyes blinked open. She shut them and tried again. Not a thing.

Knowing that trying too hard to make the unconscious surface often had exactly the opposite effect, she meandered back to the kitchen. She microwaved some of the colcannon she had made last night. The Celtic dish was one of Casey's favorites. The mashed potatoes, butter, leeks, milk, finely chopped cabbage and onion all usually tasted better to her when eaten the day after it was cooked.

When the colcannon did little to make her unconscious rise, she decided to have some cold Limerick ham. Just as she was about the slice the juniper-smoked meat, she saw an image of Jenny lying on the couch holding her head from a migraine and saying in the irritated manner an allergic reaction usually gave to her tone, "I don't care how careful everybody's been—I smell lily of the valley!"

Kate frowned intently.

There was something she had read once about lily of the valley that connected it somehow to foxglove. But she couldn't remember in what way.

She hurried to the study where she paged through *Encyclopaedia Britannica* till she read:

lily of the valley (*Convallaria majalis*): fragrant perennial herb and only species of the genus *Convallaria* of the family Liliaceae, native to Eurasia and eastern North America. Lily of the valley has nodding, white, bell-shaped flowers that are borne in a cluster on one side of a leafless stalk. The grassy leaves, usually two, are located at the base of the plant. The fruit is a red berry, and the root stock creeps horizontally below the ground. Lily of the valley is cultivated in shaded garden areas in many temperate parts of the world. The plant stems grow closely together, forming a dense mat.

Anxiously she thumbed the page but only found the next heading (lily-trotter).

Slamming the book shut she marched to the living room.

Perhaps she should try summoning another of the images that had awakened her.

She lay on the couch and gently closed her eyes. Presently she became aware that her tongue was pushing against the backs of her teeth and she allowed it to relax. In moments she could feel her jaw grow slack. Before long, her eyes floated.

But all she could envision was Jenny's contorted face as she lay holding her head, complaining about the lily of the valley.

She was on her way back to the kitchen to clean up when she remembered how lily of the valley and foxglove were connected.

She hurried to the study. From a section of the floor-to-ceiling bookcase containing Josh's collection on forensics she took down a volume entitled *Plant Poisons*, found lily of the valley and read:

> The leaves, roots, flowers and fruits contain the cardiac glycoside convallatoxin and other glycosides that act as a strong heart stimulant much like digitalis.

Her heart tripped and set to pounding. She was short of breath. She looked down on the page again:

> Symptoms can be hallucinations, vomiting, diarrhea, headache, dizziness, nausea and heart failure.

Her surging adrenaline sharpened her perceptions. She took the book under her arm and returned to her bedroom.

She had planned to wake Josh, but when she saw how the boy in his face had surfaced in his deep sleep she reconsidered.

What had she discovered, after all? Lily of the valley was as common a scent as one could find anywhere. It was used in perfume, cologne, talc, and—God knew what else. No doubt one of them—Nora, Casey, Sawyer, Josh, maybe even herself—had picked up the tiniest hint of scent on their clothing. And Jenny had been keenly aware of the odor, though no one else was.

She allowed herself a few moments of disappointment, then tried to conjure up more of the images that had awakened her.

None came.

Eventually she dozed off into a fitful sleep.

40

IN KATE'S DREAM she and Sawyer were in a men's boutique. Sawyer, dressed particularly elegantly in a black turtleneck under a dove-gray silk shirt and white flannel slacks, was choosing other turtlenecks. Each time he tried one on he stepped behind a wooden slatted screen.

After Kate had agreed enthusiastically with him about a dozen different-colored turtlenecks, she found what she felt was a lovely basque shirt. But Sawyer brushed it away when she offered it to him. Undaunted, she found a mock turtle in taupe, a color he had admired in a turtleneck that hadn't been available in his size. When she presented the mock to him he rejected it.

"But why?" she said.

She reached out and playfully tried to pull the turtleneck he was wearing away from his throat. Terrified, he avoided her grasp.

"I never want to see you again!" he shouted, then turned and stamped out of the shop.

Now, waking at nine thirty-four, Kate shook her head philosophically. Dredging up images from her unconscious had created new ones to confuse her. With less than a hundred hours before Casey had to suffer the Feebies, she was in no mood to enjoy this particular irony.

Turning over, she discovered a note in Josh's place.

Morning sweetie,
Jen and I tried to wake you but you were comatose.

In case you don't remember today is my monthly Stargazers' meeting at the Museum of Natural History. So I'll see you tonight. Jen kissed you goodbye. She needed to get home for a doctor's appointment.

Love, kisses, and myriad erotic thoughts.

P.S. Jen and I went out for assorted bagels and cream cheese and chives which are on the counter under the cupboard where we keep the wineglasses.

There in the room darkened by miniblinds she smiled at Josh's thoughtfulness.

Then she heard her father say, "Is it in bed we look for murderers now?"

"Sure Pop, haven't you heard of crimes of passion?"

"Before you were a twinkle here." He pointed at his right eye. "C'mon, time's a wasting."

She used the adjoining bathroom, then dressed in beige wide-wale cords and the lovely lilac sweater Jenny had given her for Christmas.

Lilac.

Something about the lily of the valley still disturbed her. She couldn't begin to try to think what it was before she'd even had her morning coffee.

In the kitchen she ground beans and poured water into the coffeemaker. While she waited she toasted a bagel and smeared it with cream cheese and chives.

Josh had retrieved their copy of the *Times* from the front door and, dear man, placed it right where he knew she would be having breakfast.

As she read she saw a feature story in which half a dozen well-known members of the Mystery Writers of America each had written a scenario about a fictional Widowmaker.

She threw down the paper, making crumbs scatter. Cleaning up, she wondered what was making her so short. Usually she would have delighted in such a story.

She realized she was frustrated because her hunches—her naggings—weren't allowing her her routine, which she needed for refreshment. Even her sleep was haunted by these naggings!

When she was deeply into a case for this long, the case often "talked to her"—in dreams, while she was driving, in the shower, anywhere at all. She kept pen and paper or a recorder close by for notes of these feelings.

One thing was certain: These intuitions wouldn't just go away. The best way to exorcise them was simply to surrender. Give them the fertile field in which they would bloom and ripen sooner.

With that in mind she returned to her bedroom. Purposely keeping the blinds drawn, she lay on the bed and closed her eyes. Unclenched her teeth. Wrenched her tongue away from the roof of her mouth. Concentrated on the space between her eyes.

After a long while she began to relax. Then to float. She tried once again to conjure the images that had awakened her.

At length she was able to picture Jenny on the couch complaining about the scent of lily of the valley.

Then the scene from her dream of Sawyer returned. She had tried and failed to reveal what his turtleneck was concealing on his throat.

She dragged breaths down her throat.

Next the images came fast, spinning before her sequentially like a child's flash cards:

Jenny complaining about the lily of the valley.

Sawyer's odd insistence on buying only turtlenecks.

Again and again she had the pictures flash in her mind. Faster and faster. Till at last she was reduced to intuitions.

Her mouth was dry, her pulse was leaping in her neck, she was sweating at the roots of her hair. Lily of the valley, after all, contained enough digitalis to cause heart failure. And Jenny *had* smelled it, in a room with only her, Josh, Nora, Casey, and Sawyer.

Sawyer had too much style and versatility and taste in his

dressing to restrict so vital a part of his wardrobe to turtlenecks. Perhaps there was an innocent reason. Maybe a hideous scar. No, he was certainly the type to have gone for plastic surgery.

Hard as she tried, Kate could not come to a logical conclusion.

How had Sawyer gotten to her so quickly anyway? Was it in part due to her unhappiness with the people in Rhinebeck? How much did she really know about Sawyer? It was one thing for Jenny to come up with the idea of a natural substance like foxglove instead of a manufactured digitalis. How had Sawyer arrived at the same conclusion?

What was Sawyer hiding? What might his insistence on wearing only turtlenecks have to do with that?

It was a question far too remote, like trying to call up a visceral sense of how far a light-year is.

With this, doubt found a chink and pulled itself in: "Why so many questions about Sawyer? What about the photograph he showed us all of himself with Greg Haines at Saint Bart's? His feelings for Greg? They certainly seemed real."

"Even in my day, girl," her father answered, "a good photographer could jerry up a snapshot so's your old man could be seen kicking the King of England in his keister."

"But—"

"You're almost there. Trust your gut. When you hear hoofbeats look for a horse, not a zebra. Keep asking yourself questions. There'll be an answer. There always is. I'm off."

Knowing that it sometimes helped if she wrote her intuitions down, she took a pen and pad from the nightstand and began to make notes as she thought.

She asked herself again about the connection between turtlenecks and lily of the valley.

What might hide beneath a turtleneck besides a scar? What else was on a throat, anyway, besides an Adam's apple?

Suddenly a new intuition seized her like an itch in a limb that's fallen asleep.

Why would someone want to hide his Adam's apple?

When the answer came she could feel her scalp shift, and she lunged with her entire body, clapping her hand over her mouth to keep from screaming. She realized she had bitten a small piece out of the inside of her cheek.

She made her way to the window and drew the blind open to make sure that the stand of black walnut trees was still out there.

He wore turtlenecks to hide the fact that he didn't have an Adam's apple.

Sawyer was a woman.

Her mind leapt now, racing to the shocking—and only—conclusion: Sawyer was the Widowmaker.

He had hidden his sex and fooled them all, to be close to the case. God!

"Hope I'm not disturbing you," came a disembodied voice.

She spun around although she had already recognized who it was.

"I had a ghastly morning shopping for a new tiara," Sawyer said, standing in her doorway. "How about you?"

$\triangledown$

41

SHE WONDERED IF the blood would ever return to her head and bring new oxygen so she could think and speak and come unrooted from where she stood.

"Sorry," she heard herself squeak, then cleared her throat. "Startled me, that's all." She became aware she was looking around the room for a weapon. Her eyes spied a brass lamp not more than three steps away.

"The door was open. Hope you don't mind."

When she could speak she said, "Well, I—"

"Come downstairs," he said, "and I'll make us two Bloodies guaranteed to calm you down and wake me up."

She saw him look down at the bed, where her notes and Josh's book on plant poisons lay. Her breath stopped. "Sounds interesting," she lied. She would drink transmission oil to get him—her—away from the book.

"Are you all right?" he said.

His eyes scrutinized her. She looked into his face and knew from his expression that he had seen her fear. She glanced furtively at the lamp.

And then, as if she were watching in a nightmare, she saw him sight her notes and the book. Her hands were trembling, and her ears had begun to ring. She had to dig her nails into her palm to keep her control.

To survive, she would have to be calm enough to reason with him.

She tried to take a deep breath but her diaphragm was

locked. She pushed her fist into her stomach to unlock it. Then took three deep breaths.

"Following up on foxglove, are you?"

"Yes."

"May I?" he said, looking at her notes and the book.

"I'd rather you didn't," she began, but he had already read her notes and seen his name. She saw him look at the earmarked page as if it were on fire.

A chilled sweat poured out and began running down her back.

His eyes widened and a look of comprehension flicked across his face. Finally his mouth warped into a scowl.

When he looked up he bludgeoned Kate with his eyes.

The ring of the phone cracked the air and made her lunge with her entire body.

"Don't answer it," he commanded.

Every nerve in her twanged.

He pulled up his left pants leg, where a leather sheath was strapped. He drew from the sheath an astonishingly long knife.

Her mind hurled back to the time when she had seen the Central Park Slasher's blade enter her and she'd smelled her own blood. After she'd fallen to the grass she'd felt her eyes concentrating on a ladybug, thinking it would be the very last thing she'd ever see.

Now she was breathing so fast and hard she feared she would hyperventilate and faint.

"Let it go on the machine," he ordered, pointing with the blade to the PhoneMate on the night stand. He might have been explaining something to a slow child.

The ringing gave her time to adjust her breathing, get her wind.

Finally the answering machine came on. After the beep Casey said: "It's me, guys. Rack up one more. This one's more dangerous than a six-pack of Bundys."

Kate knew it was a combination of adrenaline and lack of oxygen that had put sparkling lights in front of her eyes. She patted her face noiselessly to bring blood. Then reached further than she'd ever had to reach for her voice.

"The photograph of you and Greg was faked, wasn't it?"

"Playing detective right up to the end. Well, aren't you the good little Girl Scout. Yes, it was done by an expert. Now a dead expert."

Kate tried to swallow with no success.

Despite herself she couldn't keep from staring, searching for the woman, the Widowmaker in him. Finally, her eyes fastened on where a woman's breasts would be.

"Oh these," Sawyer said, pointing to his flat chest, and in one mercurial movement he tore off his jacket and pulled his turtleneck out of his pants up to his neck. There was a sleeveless, collarless white dickey underneath that appeared starched to the consistency of wood.

Sawyer undid the nylonlike cords that held it in place and lifted it. A woman's breasts were held flattened down by strips of flesh-colored tape.

Kate waited, concentrating so hard she feared he might guess what she planned.

When he began to retie the cords of the dickey, she lunged to her right, grabbed the brass lamp, and threw it at Sawyer.

Instinctively he caught the lamp, letting go of the knife. Kate ran toward the door. As she passed him he turned and caught her left ankle with his right foot. She fell onto her stomach, knocking the air from her. As she gasped she could feel Sawyer standing over her. When she turned and looked up she saw that he had retrieved the knife. Her sphincter muscle nearly failed.

Please make it quick and painless!

▽

42

THE PHONE RANG, startling her. She hadn't thought she was capable of feeling anything more.

Soon she heard Casey's dear gruff tones.

"We made the body. Paul Zahler. Got a girlfriend, Nina Benanti, who we can't find. Could be something. Call me, will ya. I'm dying over here."

Nina felt herself trying to rise out of Sawyer's head. The facts about what he had done to her Paul were like the lantern fish that dwelt in the deepest depths of the ocean. When you brought them to the surface they exploded, covering you with a bilious goo that you couldn't wash away.

Sawyer willed the pathetic twit down deeper inside his body.

Suddenly Kate's head was yanked back by the hair, and when the icy blade was pressed against her throat, her bladder voided and she swung both her elbows back frantically.

When Nina climbed out this time the entire world had grown grotesque. And she rose to the frayed edge of herself, not knowing where she ended and the others in her began.

"Paul. The sweetest, dearest—and all those other dead men." It was as if she had awakened as a shark with the bleeding leg of a sailor dripping down into her throat.

Kate heard the woman's voice. She felt as though she were a phonograph record from which a stylus had been lifted, leaving her spinning. She felt the blade cut her skin. *HolyMaryMotherofGod.* She squeezed her eyes shut.

Waited.

What was he waiting for?

"Don't get your clit in an uproar," Carmina said.

Nina felt she had appeared organically out of her very thoughts.

"It was me who saved you from Paul, not Sawyer. Me you should be thanking, you ungrateful cunt."

Kate had heard a second woman speak. Her voice was dark and cruel, unlike the first one.

Sawyer was a multiple!

A sound had begun inside Nina. It came from so deep it was as though it had originated in her spleen. It rose up in her, resonating relentlessly until, lips curled back, teeth gnashed, face turned volcanic red, she finally emitted a cry she'd held back since that first time her father had taken her on her bedroom floor with her face staring into the eyes of her Chatty Cathy doll.

Without Paul all she had left was her old existence. And she couldn't live with the fact that a part of her had killed the man she'd loved most.

She raised the blade high above her head.

Kate heard herself scream and fall to the floor and she knew she was dead.

A moment passed. Then two. Slowly the thought entered her mind: There was no longer a blade pressed to her throat. No grip yanking back her hair.

She pushed herself up but both her legs gave way and she fell to her knees.

When she turned she saw that the Widowmaker had plunged the knife in to the handle between the taped-down breasts.

▽

Epilogue

A WEEK AFTER Nora and Casey had returned from honeymooning in Ireland, they and Jenny weekended at Kate and Josh's new home in Williamsville, a suburb of Buffalo.

This night Jenny had invited the new man in her life for dinner. An intensely bearded medical student at UB, Nicholas nonetheless had the smile of a boy. Kate and Josh liked him instantly.

After a dinner of organic lamb stew topped off with barn brack cake Nora had brought back from County Armagh, they drank coffee and teas.

Shortly Jenny began tapping her waterglass with a bread knife. When she had everyone's attention she pulled a gaily wrapped green box from her purse and handed it to Nora.

"But you've already given us a wedding gift."

"Well," Jenny said, "think of this as an after-wedding gift."

Casey said, "Is that at all related to an after-dinner drink?"

All broke into laughter except Jenny's date, who smiled the smile of the bewildered.

Casey had lost twenty-eight pounds since his retirement and—he was quick to tell them—hadn't had a drink in four months, five days, and eighteen hours.

"—From Jenny, Kate and Josh," Nora was saying, "Caseys Go Bragh."

She held up a Waterford crystal bell for her husband to see. Then she read the enclosed card: " 'It's an old Irish tradition to give a bell at the time of a wedding. The bell affords good luck. And if at any time during the marriage there is discord, the ancient Irish remedy for lovers' quarrels is to ring this special bell and break the spirit of discontent and renew again the spirit of love.' "

Nora looked up and smiled at Josh and Kate. "It's lovely."

"Amen and thanks," Casey said.

Kate suggested that they take their teas and coffees out on the porch since it was such a balmy night.

Outside it was indeed lovely—with a starless, empty sky and not even a slice of the moon visible.

"Looks like eternity took the night off," Nicholas said.

"Not quite," Josh said, smiling, and held out his arm invitingly for the young man to look through the telescope at the end of the porch.

In moments Nicholas looked up in astonishment. "I'm used to electron microscopes, but this takes my breath away."

"Still does mine, too," Josh said.

Two hours later Nora and Casey had gone up to bed and Jenny and Nicholas had gone for a walk.

Josh adjusted the telescope and beckoned Kate over.

As she gazed he said, "Someday all of this will be yours."

"Funny man," she said. "It already is."